'I don't want h

Ben stood to take he[...]
she felt his body ag[...]
that she had never loved him as she did now.

His next words came as a shock. 'Jo, I can't help you. You must see this is something that you must do for yourself.'

'But what do *you* want for me?'

'You know that very well. Above all, I want you to be happy. But only you can decide where that happiness comes from.'

'Will you stay here when Harry comes?'

'I don't think that's a good idea so I'll go now. Jo, you know this is the hardest thing I've ever done in my life?'

She thought about it a moment. Looked at his stricken face. 'Yes, I know that,' she said. 'But before you go just hug me again.'

He held her, and she tried to draw power from his body, know that he could be hers. If she had the strength to claim him.

NURSING SISTERS

**Nursing might be their first love—
but it won't be their last…**

Kate and Jo Wilde are dedicated to each other as sisters
and dedicated to their nursing careers. They've both
never been short of admirers, but Kate has never
looked and finds it a problem when love finds her.
While Jo, always the home bird, open to stability, love
and marriage, finds herself jilted at the altar. Both have
the strength of character to fight their way through
their disappointments and dilemmas to find their own
kind of happiness.

**A FULL RECOVERY is Jo's story
and the final part of this moving duo.**

A FULL RECOVERY

BY

GILL SANDERSON

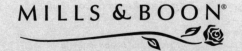

MILLS & BOON®

For John Moreton—
A true counsellor.

*First published in Great Britain 2001
Harlequin Mills & Boon Limited,
Eton House, 18-24 Paradise Road, Richmond, Surrey TW9 1SR*

© Gill Sanderson 2001

ISBN 0 263 82681 3

*Set in Times Roman 10½ on 12 pt.
03-0801-47962*

*Printed and bound in Spain
by Litografia Rosés, S.A., Barcelona*

CHAPTER ONE

KNEELING in the garden wasn't a good idea. It made her leg hurt. Stiffly, Jo Wilde climbed to her feet and felt the blood rush through the damaged limb. For a moment it hurt even more. In fact, it was hard to remember a time when her leg hadn't hurt. Still, a complex fracture of the tibia and fibula—the two great bones of the lower leg—wasn't easy to get over.

But that had been seven weeks ago. After her fortnight's stay in hospital she had religiously followed all the instructions of her physiotherapist, resting when told and then working like a demon on her exercises. She *deserved* to be fit again. In fact, she hardly limped at all now, and only occasionally did the pain get too bad. She was ready to start work again. Or was she?

One thing was certain. Work was all that was left in her life now.

She looked at her garden with a little pride. In the June sunshine it appeared quite attractive. All her neighbours in the new little estate had worked hard on their gardens, too, but she thought hers was as good as any. It was hard to remember that just three months ago they had all been wildernesses of clay and weeds. Three months ago! Life had been different then.

Painfully, she stooped to pick up the bunch of flowers she had cut and walked back into the house. The flowers were a welcome. Her twin sister, Kate, would arrive from America in half an hour, accompanied by her new fiancé Steve. Jo was really looking forward to seeing them both, but she knew it would be a shock. Seeing the couple so happy, it was certain to remind her of how happy she had been herself not so long ago. In retrospect, so much joy was bound to have an ending.

Eight weeks ago when Jo had welcomed Kate into this house, she could remember how excited they'd both been. Kate was to have been her chief bridesmaid when she'd married Harry Russell. But Harry had jilted her. A week before the wedding he had backed out. And only Kate's comfort and support had kept her sane.

Jo had forced herself to think about it, to accept it. If Harry hadn't wanted to marry her, then it had been good to find out in time. But had he had to do it so cruelly? Just to disappear, with a message left for her with his friend? It had hurt her so much. The tears came to her eyes. The pain inside her was still raw.

Her leg needed exercise. She forced herself to walk round the house, finding vases for the flowers, making sure that the already tidied house was super-tidy.

But the work did no good. She couldn't stop herself remembering. The last time Kate had returned she had been fancy-free, while Jo had been looking forward to married life. Now it was Kate who would soon get married, and she, Jo, was fancy-free. She was returning to her career as a theatre nurse. She had learned there would be no man for her ever again. It hurt too much. Yes, she had learned.

She worked as a theatre nurse for Andrew Kirk, the consultant surgeon for the neurological department. Once she had been called in on an emergency, an eighteen-year-old boy who had skidded and fallen from his motorcycle. His head had struck the edge of the pavement, causing a depressed stellate fracture of the skull. There had been cerebrospinal fluid leaking from his ears when he'd arrived in Theatre and Andrew had looked angry. 'We'll do what we can,' he had told the weeping mother, 'but quite frankly he's in a very serious state.'

The lad had died on the table, and Andrew had been incandescent with rage. 'He wasn't wearing a helmet,' he'd snarled. 'His mother said he didn't like them. Apparently he's had one accident already—skull fracture again, but just a hairline one. Wearing a helmet would have saved his life. Why won't people learn, Jo, why won't people learn?' Andrew hated to lose someone.

Well, she had learned. Never again. There would be no more men, no more declarations of love for her. She would stick to her career.

Kate had phoned from Las Vegas, where she'd been holidaying with Steve. Jo hadn't heard from her for a fortnight. This had been a deliberate policy. After the love and the care Kate had shown her since Harry had left, they had both decided that it would be as well if Jo stayed at home and learned to live on her own. But it had been good to hear from her sister at last.

Kate's voice had been cautious. 'We didn't want to spring this on you, big sister, but Steve and I are going to get married. I'm giving up roaming round the world. I want to settle in Kirkhelen and be a GP's wife.'

Jo managed to congratulate her sister, and said honestly that she thought they'd be very happy together.

And she *was* happy for Kate, but she recognised the concern in her sister's voice.

'You're worried how I'll feel about it, aren't you?'

'Just a bit,' Kate admitted. 'There must be a contrast with the last time I came home. Then you were getting married and—'

'Kate, I'm glad you're getting married and I think Steve is a lovely man. Now, don't worry about me, I'll be all right.'

'Course I'll worry about you. That's what sisters are for. Now, tell me honestly, how are you?'

'I'm good. Andrew wants me back at work next week and I'm looking forward to it. He says I'm only to scrub for short ops to start with—I can move OK but standing still for a long time makes my leg ache. But it's getting better.'

'I think work will be good for you. I can still live with you, can't I?'

'Of course you can! But when are you going to get married? Have you fixed a date yet?'

'No date, and I don't think it will be for a while. Plenty of time to make decisions when we come home.'

Firmly, Jo said, 'If you're putting off the wedding because you're worried about my feelings—don't bother. I'll be so happy to see you married. Then I'll know I've got you where I want you—here at home instead of wandering round the world.'

'Could be. I must say, I'm rather looking forward to settling down. See you Saturday, then.'

It wasn't a complete shock—Jo had wondered if something like this might happen when Steve and Kate went on holiday. But it did change things. Kate would be local—but she would be married.

Outside she heard a car draw up. There was the quick beep of the horn. She opened the front door. Kate and Steve were hauling their bags out of the back of the car. The driver was Vanessa, Steve's practice manager, and she gave Jo a quick wave. And as the car drew away, Jo walked forward to greet her sister—and her sister's new fiancé.

As twins, they knew how each other might feel. Now Jo saw Kate looking at her warily, still not sure of her welcome.

'I'm all right,' Jo said. 'I'm not an invalid any more. Now, come and kiss me. I've missed you.' It was good to hold Kate, to feel the firm body so like her own.

Then she turned to Steve. Steve had been—for that matter, still was—Harry's cousin. They were wildly different in character. But there was still some family resemblance—something about the body, the angle of head and neck that reminded her piercingly of her lost fiancé. She would have to get used to it.

She threw her arms round him, hugged him. 'Welcome to the family,' she said. 'There's no one I would rather Kate married. I'm happy for both of you.' And she realised this was true.

'Come on in, the kettle's on and I'll make us some tea. But first let me see your ring.'

Once again she saw the doubt flash in Kate's eyes. 'It's OK,' Jo said, 'I've got my old engagement ring upstairs, I'm just waiting for the chance to give it back. But I want to see yours.'

It was a lovely ring, a heart-shaped ruby with diamonds round it. But there was a twist in her heart as she thought of Harry.

'You want to give your ring back?' asked Steve. 'Has Harry been in touch at all? Have you heard anything about him or from him?'

'Nothing,' she said flatly. 'And that's the way I want it. In time I'll sell the ring if he doesn't ask for it.'

But she felt a stab of loneliness inside her. She knew that Kate's love for her wouldn't diminish. But now no longer was it the two of them against the world. Kate now had Steve to love as well. 'Leave your bags in the hall and sit down,' she said. 'I've done some sandwiches, then perhaps you'd like a bath each. Can you stay a while, Steve?'

'For a while. Then I'd better get back to the surgery to see how they've coped without me.'

'We've brought you a couple of presents...' said Kate.

It was good to have Kate back. But now she had to get back to work herself. That Sunday night the still jet-lagged Kate went to bed quite early. Jo did the exercises to strengthen and make her leg supple, had a bath and sat quietly for a while. Tomorrow she was back in Theatre.

She wondered if her confidence had gone. But how could it? She had been a theatre nurse for many years, and knew she was generally considered to be a good one. She closed her eyes. The last major op she had scrubbed for had been the removal of a meningioma— a non-malignant tumour in the membranes that enclosed and protected the brain. She would go through it, stage by stage. Remind herself of what she did.

In the neurological theatre there had been herself, the anaesthetist, Andrew Kirk and Ben Franklin, the new senior registrar. There had also been a second nurse, the senior house officer and a couple of students. She had worked with Andrew a lot. The two of them were part of a tight team—each able to guess what the other was thinking, doing.

She hadn't seen much of Ben Franklin, but she thought he was friendly and she knew he was competent. However, when he had joined the team, all her spare thoughts had been for her impending marriage.

In fact, she remembered that Ben *had* made an impression on her. Andrew was forceful, dynamic—just being with him was sometimes tiring. It was part of being one of the best neurosurgeons in the North of England. But Ben was calmer. As they had gone into the theatre Andrew had been preparing himself in his own way for the long operation. He had become curt, brusque. Ben had taken time to notice that one of the students had been nervous. He'd talked to the girl, and had managed to calm her. Afterwards he hadn't joined Andrew and Jo for lunch, but had sat with the students and talked them through what had taken place. He was a kind, thoughtful man, she realised.

The patient was an elderly man. He had been to his GP complaining of impaired speech and understanding. The GP had referred him to hospital. After careful examination, a computerised tomographic scan and magnetic resonance imaging—commonly known as CT and MRI scans—had shown up the cause and the site of the problem. A tumour.

The anaesthetised patient was wheeled into the operating theatre, his head already shaved. Andrew stared at the scans of the skull on the wall, then marked the area he intended to cut through.

Jo handed him a scalpel. Andrew cut through the skin to the perioseum, the thin membrane covering the skull. There was plenty of blood. They handled the suction together and used electric diathermy to seal the numerous small bleeding blood vessels.

Then Andrew carefully made a series of small burr holes in the skull and passed a soft metal guide from one hole to the next. A fine wire saw—a Gigli saw— was then passed along the channel made by the guide. Using handles at each end of the wire, Andrew then sawed through the bone. He repeated this procedure until the flap of bone was free and could be pulled upwards.

The tumour was now visible, pressing down into the brain itself under the pia mater and the arachnoid membranes. Andrew cut through these, then started on the delicate job of identifying and tying off the many blood vessels supplying the tumour. Only then could the tumour be gently cut away and disposed of. Jo watched, as she had so often.

Soon the job was finished. Andrew closed, stitching back the dura mater, replacing the bone flap and securing it with a few lengths of fine wire. The incision in the skin of the skull was closed with catgut stitches.

Not once had Andrew or Ben asked her for an instrument. Whatever they needed she had known, had put in their hands. It was her job and she was good at it. Everyone said so.

So that was it. She remembered everything she did,

everything that needed doing. She could do it again. The palms of her hands were clammy, her forehead was beaded with perspiration. Her leg hurt, and she realised she had been unconsciously tensing the muscles. But, she told herself, she would be all right.

And if she wasn't, she knew that Ben would help. Interesting, that she felt she could rely on Ben, a comparative newcomer, rather than her old friend Andrew. She remembered Ben looking at her over his surgical mask, nothing of his face visible but those gorgeous blue eyes. All she could see was the eyes, but she knew he was smiling. She would be all right.

Tomorrow, she knew, wouldn't be too hard. Andrew had said that they'd start with something small, an operation that didn't go on too long. She would be all right with them. She was Jo Wilde, known as a good theatre nurse. She had better be good. From now on it was going to be her entire life.

Jo and Kate got up early together next morning. Both were going to the hospital, Jo to work, Kate to make enquiries about a full-time job in the accident and emergency department. She had been told that there was one waiting for her if she wanted it.

They parted in the car park. Kate kissed Jo. 'You'll be OK,' she said. 'You're among friends and you got an excellent reputation as a nurse. See you for lunch?'

Jo had left the hospital last as a patient, now she was returning as a nurse. Strange, how being a patient for a while altered your view of a hospital completely. She'd thought she'd been a reasonably sympathetic nurse before, but now she'd experienced the feelings of pain, dependence, gratitude and sometimes sheer fear that being a patient could bring on. She knew she'd be a better nurse for it.

She felt much better by the time she reached the little waiting room where staff relaxed before they entered the neurological theatre complex. Many people shouted hello to her, asked her how she had been, said they were glad she was back—porters, security personnel, X-ray technicians, ward clerks, office workers, as well as doctors and nurses. It made her feel good, she could relax. She was among friends.

Waiting for her was Ben. He was sitting—lying almost—in his greens, feet on the occasional table, a mug of coffee balanced on his chest. 'Welcome back, Jo,' he said amiably. 'Fresh coffee in the pot. Sit down and have an energising shot of caffeine.'

He didn't leap to his feet and offer to pour her one. She liked that, liked the casual approach. He was acting as if today was just an ordinary day—for her and for him. That was what she needed. She got herself a coffee and sat opposite him. 'You're early,' she said. 'I couldn't sleep—what's your excuse?'

He waved his mug gently. 'I know you're always the first one here. I wanted to have a couple of words with you before the gang arrived. Ask you something and give you the chance to say no privately.'

'Say no to what?' The words didn't come out as she had intended. She sounded defensive, upset even. This wasn't the way she wished to behave.

Ben, however, didn't seem to notice. 'I have a favour to ask you. Quite frankly, I'm a bit lost. A bit frightened even. I need someone to hold my hand—metaphorically speaking, of course.'

He lifted his hand and looked at it gloomily. She

had to laugh. 'I don't think I've ever seen anyone look less frightened than you do right now.'

The greens he wore were shapeless, of course, but they couldn't hide the muscular body. His very stillness suggested confidence, a quiet reliance on his own abilities. And those piercing blue eyes!

Perhaps for the first time she looked at Ben as a man, not a colleague. Apart from the eyes, his face wasn't striking at first. His dark hair was longish, but not ridiculously so. In fact, it looked rather curly. After the eyes, the first thing that struck her was his smile. It was friendly, inviting confidences. He smiled a lot, she realised. And the rest of his features fitted him well. It was a welcoming face.

Then it struck her—Ben Franklin was a very attractive man. And she didn't need thoughts like this. She was finished with men.

'How can I help?' she asked abruptly.

He didn't seem to notice the coldness in her voice. 'I've been asked to give a talk to something called the Riston Ladies' Lunch Club. This coming Friday, in fact. Just a half hour talk on the work of a neurological surgeon. Apparently Andrew's wife is a friend of the chairman. Andrew was going to do it, but he's off doing something important in London. So I've been drafted in, and I thought you might like to come and help me.'

'No, I couldn't! I mean, they want to hear from you, not me. You're the surgeon.' The last thing she wanted was to have to appear in public.

'It's not really heavy stuff,' he went on placidly. 'The last two speakers were a man who has sailed the Atlantic single-handed and a woman who's a public health official. And the club has organised a couple of very generous collections for the hospital benevolent fund.'

'You're trying to blackmail me!' she accused.

'Of course. I'm deep, devious and an evil person at heart.'

She had to giggle. It would be hard to envisage anyone less like an evil person than the relaxed man in front of her.

He went on, 'There is a serious point to what I'm trying to do. I believe—as does Andrew—that our work in Theatre should be seen as a joint effort. What you do, what the anaesthetist does, what the second nurse does—all these skills are interrelated. So I want to talk for fifteen minutes and then I want you to talk for fifteen minutes.'

'Oh, I agree with what you say. You are deep and devious.'

'Discovered at last. I may add as an extra bribe that we get a free lunch and that we can share the book token that we'll be given.'

Jo thought for a moment. This was the last thing she'd expected when she'd walked into this room. 'I've never been asked to speak in public before,' she said. 'I'm not sure I'm up to it. You know my private life recently has been a bit...troubled.'

'Yes, I know. But if you can walk into that operating theatre and do the things you do there, then speaking to a set of interested ladies should be a lot easier. You're a highly skilled professional, Jo. I want you to celebrate that.'

She felt a warm glow at his obviously sincere words. Yes, she was a highly skilled professional. 'It's just that I've never done anything like this,' she said. 'I wouldn't want to let you down. I'd be…a bit frightened.'

'You'd have nothing to fear but fear itself. An American President said that. And if you wanted, we could work together on your speech.'

It was an interesting thought. And it might take her mind off things. 'OK,' she said, 'I'll do it. But you do twenty minutes and I'll do ten. I take it Andrew has arranged for us to be off that afternoon.'

'All taken care of,' Ben assured her. 'Tonight you can think about what you'd like to say, make a few notes, and tomorrow we'll run over what you've decided.'

He was quite forceful in his own way, Jo thought. It wasn't obvious, but he got what he wanted.

'I'll think of something,' she said, 'and then—'

'Time you were back, Nurse Wilde. You're part of my team. Only you understand what I'm thinking before I do myself. Are you going to be all right?'

Andrew was in the doorway. Tough, ready for work. For the past seven weeks he had been her friend, and no one could have been more concerned for her welfare. But for the next few hours he was going to be her boss, and things would be different. It was typical of him that he wanted this made clear.

'I'm going to be fine, Andrew. Not an invalid any more. I'm a theatre nurse.'

'That's good. Let's scrub up and get the show started, then. Ben, this first case is quite interesting…'

CHAPTER TWO

'YOUR notes are fine,' Ben told Jo. 'You don't need too much written down, just something to remind you of what you're going to say next. Remember, keep your head up and look proud. Look proud and you'll feel it.'

'But I'm still nervous!'

'So am I. But we both know that your rehearsal went really well. Jo, you've got nothing to be frightened of, you're going to knock them in the aisles.'

It must be his voice. It was warm, comforting, it gave her confidence. When he said something would happen she knew that what he said was true.

'Knocking them in the aisles isn't the idea,' she told him. 'Far too physical. I've made enquiries. The Riston Ladies' Club is a very respectable group. I wouldn't be surprised if some of them didn't wear hats throughout the meal.'

He glanced at her casually. 'Perhaps so. But I'll be more surprised if any of them look as good as you do, Jo. That suit is really something else.'

The suit *was* something else. When her sister had heard that Jo was giving a talk in the very upmarket village of Riston, she had insisted that Jo get out the suit that had been bought for her going-away after the wedding. Kate had bought it for her in Las Vegas. It was a blue silk trouser suit and Jo had never worn it.

'I paid a lot of money for this,' Kate had said, 'so

I want to see it worn. This is the perfect opportunity. Wear it and you'll look stunning. If you look good, you'll feel good, and you'll sound good. Now, try it on.'

It *was* a lovely suit. When she'd put it on Jo had realised that she had spent too much time recently slopping round in casual clothes. With a simple white blouse the suit had looked stunning.

'You've lost a bit of weight,' Kate had said critically, pulling at the loose waistband, 'but it doesn't show. Now you're working you'll need feeding up and more exercise.'

Now Jo was sitting with Ben in the little coffee-room adjoining their theatre. Usually they sprawled here in their shapeless greens, too tired to worry about how they looked. It gave her a vague shock to see Ben dressed so smartly.

'You look every inch the up-and-coming surgeon yourself,' she told him. He wore a dark grey suit, an immaculate white shirt, sober tie and shoes polished like twin mirrors. Somehow this complete formality didn't gel with what she knew of his relaxed personality. Only the sleepy smile and the unruly, rather long hair reminded her that this was the usual Ben.

When he ran his clinics she knew that he wore clothes that were a bit less formal—usually a darker shirt and a floral tie. He wanted people to have confidence in him, but not be intimidated.

But now she had to admit that he looked good.

'This isn't the real me,' he told her. 'I want to be an up-and-coming but scruffy surgeon.'

'Scruffy is something that you are not. Let's settle for…casual?'

'I'll accept casual. With perhaps a touch of nonchalant?'

'I draw the line at nonchalant. Sometimes I think you're very chalant.'

They both laughed. She felt at ease with Ben. Somehow he had just slid into her life, become a friend without her really noticing him. When they'd first met, some three months before, she had been thinking of nothing but Harry and her soon-to-come wedding. She remembered having thought vaguely that Ben was a pleasant man. He had been easy to work with, less abrasive in Theatre than Andrew could be, but a very competent surgeon. He would become a friend, like others in the tightly knit team.

Then she had been jilted, had broken her leg, had withdrawn into her shell, thinking of nothing but herself. Ben had been there, but that had been all. Now that she had started work, it was time to be aware of other people.

She supposed Ben was handsome, but that didn't really matter. No one remained impressed just by Ben's good looks. His piercing blue eyes and dark brown hair were just there, part of the overall relaxed Ben. He had an odd relaxed manner, even a relaxed walk, as if he had never in his life been in a hurry.

When she worked with him in a clinic she noticed that patients confided in Ben at once—they seemed to feel better after just talking to him. He inspired confidence. If she had to give a talk, she was glad it was with Ben.

They were meeting for a quick chat before driving out to Riston to give their joint talk. At first she had been nervous, had regretted agreeing to come with him. She hadn't wanted to expose herself to the scrutiny of a room full of women. Riston wasn't too far away, and some of them might have heard about her and her cancelled wedding.

But somehow Ben had reassured her, had told her that all would be well. 'The all-important thing is the first three sentences,' he had said. 'You need them clear, loud and confident. After that, the talk will look after itself. Now, write them down, then say them to me.'

They had rehearsed, in this little room. 'Good afternoon. My name is Jo Wilde and I'm a theatre nurse—popularly known as a scrub nurse. Without a scrub nurse a surgeon just wouldn't be able to cope. Mine is an important job and it has to be done well.'

'Don't you think it sounds a bit, well, arrogant?' she had asked.

'No. It sounds confident and it sounds true. And it is true, isn't it?'

And now she was, well, not exactly confident, but at least not too worried.

It was time to go. Ben led her down to the hospital car park to what looked like an ordinary little grey car. He drove sedately out of town, and then when they got onto the main road her shoulders were pressed back into the seat as the car roared forward.

She looked at him in surprise. 'That's a lot of power for such a little car,' she said.

'Little car, big engine,' he said. 'It pleases me.'

They moved fast but not dangerously—he was obviously a skilful driver. The car was a lot like Ben, she thought, an apparently simple exterior but an awful lot inside.

The Riston Ladies' Lunch Club met at the Hind
Hotel, an old coaching inn in the centre of the village.
They were met by the President, who *was* wearing a
hat. Jo had no great idea what the meal consisted of,
she was nervous again. But she noticed that Ben managed to chat urbanely to the rest of the people on their
table, and this made up for her silence.

His talk was good. It was both serious and comic,
talking a little about the problems surgeons had to face
but emphasising how much techniques were improving, how research was constantly finding new ways of
doing things. Jo could see that he had gone down well.

Then it was her turn. She remembered what Ben
had told her—the first three sentences, not too fast,
but clear, loud and confident. She spoke them and after
that all was well. She found herself gaining in confidence.

Jo, too, was generously applauded. Then it was time
for questions, and there were plenty. Obviously she
and Ben had aroused considerable interest. Most of the
questions were for Ben, but more than a few for herself. She felt quietly proud of herself.

The President stood, said there was time for one last
question. A cheerfully smiling lady stood and said to
Jo, 'You're not wearing any rings. I presume that
you're neither married nor engaged. What is it like,
working with handsome young men like Dr Franklin
all the time?'

Fortunately there was quite some laughter at this
question and it gave Jo a little breathing space. She
bowed her head as if thinking and her hands gripped
the edge of the table, hoping for support. How would
the woman have known her situation? she wondered.

Then pride reasserted itself. Common sense told her that the woman had meant no harm. It had been an innocent question, innocently meant. And things had gone so well so far. She would *not* show that she was upset.

Jo glanced at Ben. He was looking at her calmly. He must have known how the question had thrown her, but he wasn't worried. Instinctively she knew that he had confidence in her. That thought gave her strength.

Lifting her head, she managed to smile and said, 'Well, as a matter of fact, I love it. It's wonderful. What other job gives you the chance to work with a man who's dressed in pyjamas and always masked? It makes life so mysterious and exciting.'

This got a bigger laugh than ever. The President stood, she and Ben were courteously thanked and the lunch was over.

'We really have enjoyed being here,' Ben said to the President, 'but I'm afraid we must get back to work.' He stood to escort Jo out of the room.

It was a quality—or a skill—that Jo had noticed in him before. If something difficult needed doing, Ben would do it quickly, unobtrusively and without upsetting a single person. Somehow he led her through the room of women, smiling, nodding, promising to return. Jo didn't have to say a thing. And in no time they were back in his car, driving out of Riston.

He knew better than to say anything. Jo sat there, trying to be calm, trying to contain the ungovernable emotions that raged within her. She hadn't wanted to give this talk, she hadn't wanted to be made to face a crowd of confident women, all—or most—with husbands. She had wanted to be left alone. And just when she'd thought she was getting a little peace of mind, a little self-confidence back, someone had raked across her lacerated feelings. The fact that it had been done unconsciously, without any spite meant, if anything made things worse.

She tried, she held on, but it was no good. After five minutes the tears came and she buried her face in her hands, sobbing as if her heart were broken.

The car slowed, turned into a layby and stopped. They were well into the country by now. Vaguely she was aware of a hedgerow beside her. She could hear birds singing, smell the heat on the corn in the fields.

Still Ben said nothing. He took one of her hands and held it in his. With his other hand he stroked her hair, his touch as gentle as a baby's. How did her know that this was the quickest way to calm her?

After a while the outburst left her and she grew quieter. As always happened when she felt she had lost control like this, she began to feel both ashamed and resentful. Why did it have to happen when he was there? But for some reason she worried less about showing her feelings to Ben than she would have to most people.

'I'm sorry,' she muttered. 'I feel a fool now. It's just that…I've got out of being good with people.'

'No need. You're with a friend. You did well there, Jo. I thought we were a great team. In the theatre and on the public speaking circuit. Jo and Ben. Sound well together, don't they?'

'Yes, well…' She realised she was pleased by his small compliment. But she went on, 'What was that about having to get back to work? I thought we had the rest of the day off?'

'We're certainly not going back to hospital. Have you got any plans?'

'I'd like you to take me home, please.'

He wound down his window even further, and the scents of summer filled the car even more. She wondered where they were—this was a quiet country lane.

He said, 'I could take you home, but I'll bet you'll just sit there on your own, worrying about things. Not really a good idea. We've got three hours or so to spare so let's play truant. Why don't you spend the time with me?'

She looked at him doubtfully. 'Spend the time with you?'

'Just a couple of friends doing nothing much together. We've worked quite hard this lunchtime. All that eating, drinking and talking takes it out of you. Why not just relax a while?'

The idea of just relaxing was foreign to Jo. She hadn't 'just relaxed' for weeks. Her first inclination was to say that she'd rather be taken home. But the prospect of spending even more time in those rooms where she had moped so long—no, she'd do as he'd suggested. 'All right,' she said, 'let's do that. I'm in your hands.'

'Good.' He reached into the glovebox and took out a handful of tissues. 'Rub your face over with these,' he said.

The tissues were impregnated with sweet oil or cologne. She rubbed her face and her wrists with them and instantly felt refreshed. 'I feel better now,' she said.

He drove her gently through country lanes and she was content just to sit there, enjoying the heat of the summer sun, the smells of the countryside and the sight of the fields and woods beside them. For a while she wouldn't think. She would just be.

They drove over a hump-backed bridge, crossing a canal, and there in front of them was a pub, the Waterside Inn. He turned into the car park, and she looked at him cautiously. 'It looks very nice,' she said, 'but I don't think I could eat or drink anything more.'

'Nor could I. But the food here is good, I eat here quite a lot. Perhaps we'll try it together some other time.'

They crossed the front of the inn, looking at the people sitting outside on wooden benches. Then Ben drove through the car park towards a white gate marked MELLINGS MARINA. Behind it she could see the brightly painted tops of serried rows of narrow boats and further on the silver line of the canal. 'What are we doing here?' she asked.

'A little surprise. We agreed we wanted to relax, well, as the song says, there's no better way to relax than messing about on a river. Or, in this case, a canal. Come and see what you think.'

She looked at her expensive blue silk suit. 'This isn't the outfit I would have picked to go boating in.' she said.

'You'd pick it to wear on the *QE* 2. This boat is just as luxurious—well, almost. And quite a lot smaller, of course.'

They got out of the car and he led her along a wooden jetty, past ranks of narrow boats. She'd never really looked at a narrow boat before. Now she noticed how beautifully decorated many of them were, with intricate patterns painted round the cabin.

He noticed her looking. 'All traditional artwork,' he told her. 'Patterns date back to the nineteenth century.'

'You can carry your own garden as well,' she said, looking at a narrow boat that had a vast number of tubs of flowers on the cabin roof.

'You can, you could...but I think I'd prefer not to myself.'

He led her to the end of the jetty and stepped aboard a narrow boat called...'*Ben's Boat*?' she said incredulously.

'I'm afraid so.' He looked apologetic as he handed her down into the cockpit. 'This is my guilty secret Jo. When I was working in Birmingham I lived on this narrow boat. It was cheap, convenient and central.'

'A narrow boat in Birmingham!' Things seemed to be getting even more surreal.

'Why not? Did you know that Birmingham has got more canals than Venice?'

No, she hadn't known. But she was coming to think that there was much much more to Ben than she had realised. 'Surely not a lot of surgeons live on narrow boats?'

'Perhaps not. Perhaps I'll start a trend. Would you like to look round?'

'Yes, I'd love to.' She was intrigued. She felt that seeing someone's home gave an insight into their character. What would she learn about Ben from looking round a sixty-feet-long, six-feet-wide water-surrounded home?

He unlocked a door and she stepped down into a companionway and then into a living room. It was panelled in some light wood, with the traditional red paintings across one wall. Although small, it looked tremendously comfortable. There were small, brass-shaded lights and built-in upholstered seats that looked luxuriously soft. Lining the walls was one long continuous bookshelf. Passing through, she found herself in a galley with a dining annexe at one end. The kitchen seemed to have everything that a cook might need. Ben stopped to put on a kettle. Further on there was his bedroom, with a double bed and built-in wardrobes. Beyond that was a bathroom, not exactly large but holding everything that was necessary.

'Two more small bedrooms beyond,' he said, 'for the rare occasions when I have guests.'

The place delighted her. 'It's like a Wendy house,' she told him. 'I can think of children who would love it here.'

'What's more, if you don't like your neighbours, you can just move along. Now, that *is* magic. But most narrow-boat people tend to get along. Shall we go and sit in the cockpit now? Seems a pity to stay in while the sun's out.'

He led her back to the open stern of the boat and pulled out cushions from a locker. It was very pleasant lounging there, listening to the lap of water against the side of the boat.

She sat comfortably in the corner, kicked off her shoes and stretched her legs out along the cushions. 'First time I've worn high heels for a while,' she said. 'My feet hurt a bit.'

'Just sit and take things easy. We've got all the time in the world.'

Then it struck her. What was she doing here? This

was the first time she had been alone with a man for such a long time. What did Ben want of her? Why was he taking such trouble?

'You know all about Harry and me, don't you?' she asked flatly. 'You know about the cancelled wedding and so on.'

'I don't know much about Harry. I know about you and the broken leg.'

Her next question came before she had time to think. 'So why are you taking all this interest in me? D'you think you might catch me on the rebound?'

He had been sitting, relaxed, opposite her, his jacket by his side and his tie loosened. It seemed that nothing could worry him. He didn't seem to move, but suddenly he was a different man. Like a disturbed animal, his body was tense and his eyes flashed with anger. The change was so unexpected that she shrank away in fear.

'I'm…I'm sorry,' she mumbled. 'I shouldn't have said that. Please, don't be angry with me.'

She watched him, saw the deliberate effort he made to be calm. He lifted his arms over his head, stretched and then relaxed. She felt his eyes studying her, reassessing her, considering what to say next.

After a silence which went on and on and on, he said, 'I suppose it's natural for you to be suspicious of men. And you are, of course, a very attractive woman. I suppose there are people who might….' He shook his head in dismay. 'Jo, I find the idea of taking advantage of someone—sexually or any other way—when they're vulnerable, well, I just find it appalling.'

There was no doubting his sincerity. In the past he had always been calm, now she saw the passion inside him. She could tell by the still angry eyes, the twist to his mouth. It made her curious. 'You obviously mean that,' she said.

'I do. Very much so.'

'Is there some special reason? Are you going to tell me?'

There was a pause while he studied her again. 'Some time perhaps, but not now. You're more in need of care than I am.'

There was another pause while she thought about this.

'I don't know you very well,' she said. 'You've just got here, and I don't know much about you because I've had…other things to think about. I take it you're not married—not been married? Have you had a hard life somehow? Is that why you're so protective of vulnerable people?'

He was calmer now. She knew that the anger had left him. His body was relaxed again. But for a minute she had glimpsed a new side to Ben, a fiercer, more challenging side. It intrigued her.

He answered, 'I guess my life so far has been pretty good. In fact, if I was superstitious I'd worry a bit. Perhaps fate is saving me up for something horrific.' He smiled to show it had been a joke. 'I've always enjoyed my work and I've always got on with my colleagues.'

It was pushing things, but she was going to ask. 'What about women colleagues? Why aren't you married?' Then she blushed a little as he smiled at that question, too.

'I like women and I've had two or three relationships which might have led somewhere. Women who

I thought at first I could spend the rest of my life with. But it never happened. I like to think that when we parted there was as little pain as possible. But they weren't the cause of me being against hurting vulnerable people.'

He stood. 'That kettle will have been boiling for a while now. I'll fetch us some tea.' He stepped down into the companionway.

Now Jo had a couple of minutes to think—and quite a lot to think about. She decided that she believed him. He wasn't trying to take advantage of her, his anger at the idea had been obvious. She was relieved, of course. And, paradoxically, for the first time she now thought of him as a man.

So far Ben had been a colleague and a friend. She knew he was calm, kind, very competent. Very soon he would be as good a surgeon as Andrew, but already he had a number of interpersonal skills that Andrew would never have. He was a great pacifier in the sometimes excited atmosphere in the theatre.

And he was very attractive. The sharp blue eyes, the easy way his mouth moved when he smiled, the deep friendly voice. No wonder she had seen other nurses turning to look after him.

For such a long time she had been incapable of thinking of any man in this way. And she didn't intend to start now. She'd had it with men, she would concentrate on her work. But there was this odd feeling, almost as if she was being unfaithful to someone—or something. But who or what? Certainly not Harry. He was gone for good. She could think of any new man in any way she wanted. But she didn't want to, did she?

Ben came back with a tray on which there were biscuits, mugs and in centre place there was a big earthenware teapot. He pulled at a piece of wood which folded outwards to make a small table between them. Carefully he set down the tray.

'So what *do* you want with me?' Jo asked.

It seemed as if he needed time before answering. He busied himself, pouring the tea, handing her a biscuit, passing her the milk. But she knew this was displacement activity. He was trying to keep them both occupied while he thought of an answer.

Then, eventually, he said, 'I very much like working with you. But I can tell you're still stressed. Sometimes when we're working together in Theatre, and other times out of Theatre, when you think no one is looking. You wince as if you've just remembered something painful. Or you look sad.'

He's observant, she thought. I thought I was hiding things. But she said, 'It's natural that I wince now and again. I broke my leg. It's mending well but occasionally there's an odd twinge.'

'It's much more than that. Harry still hurts, doesn't he?'

After a pause she replied simply, 'Yes, Harry still hurts.' Just saying his name made her feel tearful.

'Have you talked to anyone about it? Have you had counselling?'

'No! I don't need counselling or any of that kind of help, I've had a bad time and I can get over it on my own!'

'Everyone needs help some time,' he told her gently. 'You, as a nurse, should know that. No one at all has tried to talk you through things?'

She thought. ''Well, you know I live with my twin sister, Kate. She helps all she can but she just hates Harry. She never knew his…good side, and I think that's important. Andrew would help but he's far too busy. Steve Russell is my GP and a friend, too, but he's too close to the situation and he…looks too much like Harry. And that sometimes puts me off. No, Ben, I'm all right. I'll manage.'

She took her mug of tea in both hands, bent down to drink from it. He recognised that she needed a moment's silence. He drank himself, looking vaguely at the sunlit wheat fields on the other side of the canal, the distant line of trees.

After a while he said, 'We've worked together for a while but you don't know me very well. I'm still not too…close to you. Would you like to talk to me about how you feel, how you're getting on? I might be able to help you.'

The invitation came as a shock—this had been the last thing she had expected. She knew he was sincere, but there could only be one possible answer.

'No, thanks, Ben. I do appreciate the offer, but I just couldn't.'

He nodded. 'You must choose, of course. But the offer is always open and all you have to do is ask. There's a lot to be said for getting things out into the open—a trouble shared really is a trouble halved.'

He wasn't looking at her, and for the moment she was pleased. His gaze was still fixed across the canal, but she knew he wasn't seeing the fields or the distant woods.

He went on, 'I knew someone—know someone—

who tried to cope on their own and was left with a lifetime of misery. And there was help available.'

'He was left with a lifetime of misery?' Jo asked.

'No, she was. It was a woman. And, no, to answer your next question, it wasn't a lover but it was someone very…dear to me.'

Now he turned his head and smiled at her. 'I think that's enough doom and gloom,' he said. 'What d'you think of living on the canal?'

She waved at the rural scene around them. 'I think this is wonderful. But what made you pick a narrow boat in the first place? You're paid quite well, you're not married or thinking of it—you could have your own bachelor flat.'

'So I could. But you're free in a narrow boat. It's like having a cottage that you can move to wherever you want, at a steady four miles per hour.'

'Hardly racing away.'

'True. But you see an awful lot at that speed. Too many people are in too much of a hurry. I like to take things easy. You learn more about people that way.'

She had to laugh at this. 'Take things easy! I've seen you operate, remember! You don't hang about.'

'Ah. Inside the brain is different. Working on the brain is like plumbing. I'm talking about the mind. When we're working inside someone's head, d'you ever wonder where the real person is hidden in there?'

'You feel the same as me,' she said. She had often wondered as they operated on blood vessels, bones, nerves, the vast complexity of a living system, just where personality was stored. Was there some kind of a ghost in there?

She watched three ducks swim past in a line, and

then threw them half a biscuit. There was an undignified splashing fight, so she threw another two pieces into the water.

Abruptly, she said, 'I'm not sure I want someone poking around in my mind. It's private.'

'There was a Jacobean love poet called John Donne. He said, "No man is an Island." No woman is either. We all need other people.'

'Why should I want to talk about my problems? I don't want other people to know how I'm managing, to be even more the talk of the hospital. I'd rather…'

Once again she saw the anger flash from his eyes. 'Jo, I'm a doctor! Even though you're not my patient, I know about confidentiality.'

'I'm sorry. I should have known better,' she said.

He didn't speak so after a while she said, 'I'd like to tell you about Harry but I just can't…I can't get used to the idea.' To her horror she found herself almost in tears. 'It's just not fair,' she said.

'Tell me about how you met him first,' Ben suggested. 'What was he like, what were you like, why did you pick him?'

She thought back. 'He was a wonderful man,' she said. 'I liked him because he thought life was a joke. Everyone laughed all time round Harry. I had been going out with his cousin, Steve, but he had to go down to London on a course and Harry came along and we…well, it just happened.'

CHAPTER THREE

IT WAS hard to go over this bit of the past. All Jo's memories were of laughter, of happiness, and yet… Still, Ben was with her and she felt safe and comforted in his presence. He made it easier for her to continue. She closed her eyes as memories eddied round her.

The past was so vivid! It wasn't retreating, as people said it would. She wasn't forgetting everything. It was still with her, part of her.

'We met first a year last Christmas,' she said, 'about twenty months ago…' Life had been simpler then.

She had gone to a hospital dance, some kind of charity ball. Steve had been with her but she hadn't exactly been his date—rather, they had gone in a crowd. She'd known she'd looked well, in a sleeveless red dress with a drop back and rather a lot of cleavage showing. But her girl friends had said how it had suited her, and it had been obvious what the men had thought, even though they'd said nothing.

She had been happy. They'd been sitting on stools, about twelve of them crammed at a table for eight, each with a paper plate full from the excellent buffet. There had been lots of casual, funny conversation.

Suddenly there had been a voice from behind her. 'There must be room for a very tiny one. I promise to be polite but I'm in trouble and I need help.'

Before she realised what was happening, a plate and a glass had been deposited in front of her. Two arms reached down and grasped the sides of the stool, picked her up bodily and moved her away from Steve then put her down again. She felt the heat of the man's body behind her, even the touch of bare skin against hers.

She turned to look. Behind her was a laughing man, his white shirt unbuttoned nearly to his waist. He kicked a stool between her and Steve and sat on it. 'Hi, cousin Steve,' he said. 'Won't you introduce me to this lovely lady?'

Steve grinned, obviously used to the man. 'Jo, this is my cousin, Harry Russell, just started work here as a junior registrar in Orthopaedics. Yes, in spite of appearances, he is a real doctor.'

Jo liked Harry at once. There was a lock of rather long hair straying down his face but he had a big smile. In fact, he was big in every way. Harry Russell was slightly larger than life.

'Harry, this is Jo Wilde, the neurology department's theatre sister,' Steve said.

'Oh, I've heard of you! You're good, the envy of every other theatre in the hospital. What would tempt you to Orthopaedics?'

'Nothing,' she said firmly. 'Too much like a rugby field. I like Neurology.'

'A pity, a pity. Steve, you lucky devil, are you and Jo an item? Am I splitting you up? Because if I am, I shall go away and cry.'

'We're very good friends,' Steve said cheerfully. 'What has driven you away from your table?'

Harry lowered his voice and glanced conspiratorially behind him. 'It's Sister Corcoran. The lady sitting next to me. She's an excellent nurse, I know, she's told me. Not married, she's told me. Still young at heart, she's told me. Aged about fifty, I worked that out for myself. Sister Corcoran is fascinated by the gall bladder and wants to share that fascination with me. So I said that you were my cousin and you'd asked me over to discuss something very important. It might even be a gall bladder. And here I am.'

By now the entire table, Jo included, was laughing at Harry's story. He was accurate about Sister Corcoran—she was known to be a bore.

Harry turned to Jo, looked at her plate and then said dolefully, 'You've got a salmon patty. There were none there when I got to the buffet and you've got two. I'll swap you a chicken leg for a salmon patty.'

'All right. Just so long as I can dip my chicken leg in your Marie Rose sauce.'

'You drive a hard bargain, woman. But I agree.'

After that he stayed with their group all night. Although he had been born in the area he had trained away and he didn't know many people in the hospital except for his cousin Steve. He danced with her, he danced with other women in the little group, he was instantly popular. Jo enjoyed his company.

The next night he phoned her and asked her to dinner the following week. 'But I don't want to upset Steve. If I'm treading on his toes, then tell me.'

She went to dinner with Harry. And after that her life turned into a roller-coaster ride.

'I loved him,' she told Ben. 'Being with him was never dull.'

'Was he good at his job?'

Jo frowned. 'I would have said yes. Certainly he was very enthusiastic about it. But I gather that at times his consultant told him off for being a bit slap-dash. He was all right in Theatre, but he hated paper-work and tried to get the ward clerks and sisters to do as much as possible.'

'What did you think of that?'

'Well, you know Andrew is absolutely determined that nothing should go wrong with his paperwork. He's absolutely meticulous, and I think a bit of that has rubbed off on me. Harry was wrong.'

She sighed. 'I guess, like all women in love, I over-looked his faults. I heard he'd had a couple of messy affairs with other women, a couple of them had been badly hurt. But he seemed to be genuinely in love with me. Then he left me, too.'

'He sounds a very attractive man,' Ben said. 'I can see why you fell for him.' He glanced at his watch. 'It's been nice talking to you here, but I think work calls. We'd better get back.'

'Aren't you going to tell me how to deal with things?' Jo asked, rather surprised.

'Certainly not. That would be very wrong. You have to make up your own mind about things. I just think it helps to talk. D'you feel just a tiny touch better?'

She thought for a moment. 'Yes,' she said, slightly surprised, 'I think I do.'

'She's not there as a convenience for you. She's a student nurse, training to be a professional. In time her contribution will be as necessary as yours. If she has to do your dirty work then you ask her, don't tell her, and you thank her afterwards. If through no fault of her own she gets something wrong, then very patiently you tell her why and how to do it right next time. Is that clear?'

There was a mumbled reply.

'I think the words you're looking for are, "Yes, Dr Franklin, sir." Now try again.'

'Yes, Dr Franklin, sir.'

'Don't forget.'

The door to the little room by the theatre had been half-open, and Jo had heard what was being said inside before she'd had a chance to walk away. Now the door was pushed fully open and a white-faced junior house officer walked out. His name was Ron Barrow. Jo had met him but hadn't been very impressed.

She walked into the coffee room. Ben was there, his usually smiling face cold, his broad shoulders hunched. She felt a tiny thrill of anxiety. This frightening person was a new Ben, one she had never met before. Then he smiled and the old Ben was back.

'I heard what you said,' she told him, 'and I passed a crying junior nurse in the corridor.'

'Barrow has got a lot to learn about how to treat people. There are some things I won't put up with. He knows that now, and God help him if he ever forgets again.'

'I think you made your point,' she said. 'He didn't look too happy. D'you want me to have a word with the nurse?'

'No. I'll do it myself. In fact, I'll do it now.' He stood, then he smiled again, and said, 'We were a good team on Friday.'

Five minutes after he'd left, Andrew walked in. 'Gather your talk went well on Friday,' he said.

'Penny says the chairman phoned, thought you were a great pair. Can I book you for any more talks?'

'I'm a scrub nurse, not a public speaker. It took a lot out of me, Andrew. Ben took me to his narrow boat afterwards to recover.'

'That man's just a water gypsy,' Andrew growled. 'Come on, let's scrub up.'

A moment later Ben joined them, as amiable as ever. They entered the theatre. 'Going to be a tricky one,' Andrew said. 'Road traffic accident. I hate them. Epidural haematoma. Woman knocked over, hit her head on the kerb, unconscious for five minutes. Because she felt quite lucid afterwards, she didn't feel the need to go to the doctor. Went to bed in the afternoon, no one knew she was bleeding into the brain. Husband tried to wake her to have a cup of tea, found she wasn't asleep, she was in a coma. Fortunately he had the sense to send for an ambulance. Let's see if we can do anything for her.'

Andrew had a management meeting and left as soon as he'd changed. Ben and Jo sat in the coffee room, legs sprawled, heads lolling on the cushions. They needed a rest. 'A difficult one,' Ben said, 'but a good job well done. It still gives you a thrill, doesn't it?'

She nodded. 'Yes, it does. Nothing in the world gives a better thrill.'

'Nothing?'

'Nothing,' she said flatly. 'Now my life's going to be dedicated to work. I told you that.'

'I'll have to persuade you that there are other things in life. A good hobby perhaps—how about needlework?'

'I think I'll stick to gardening,' she said.

Both were tired, their conversation just a means of reminding each other that they were human. They both needed casual companionship.

After a while he said, 'if you've got an evening free this week you could come out on the narrow boat with me. Go along the canal for a mile or two. We could talk a bit more if you wanted.'

'You do take it out, then? You're not moored there permanently?'

'I pay monthly for the mooring at the marina. But I often do go for little trips. It's easier with two on board. I'll show you how to operate the locks. How about Friday again?'

There was nothing Jo had to do on Friday. In fact, apart from work, there was nothing she had to do at all. 'Why are you doing this?' she asked. 'I can't be much fun as a companion.'

'I hope it'll help you,' he said calmly. 'If you like to think of it that way, perhaps I'm giving a little back.'

'Giving what back?'

Ben seemed to think for a minute, then he said, 'Just small acts of kindness that people have offered me from time to time. Perhaps I'll help you, perhaps not. But, whatever it is, I'll have tried.'

Small acts of kindness, she thought to herself. A feeling of great desolation fell on her. It wasn't him or what he had said. This feeling of emptiness came without any prompting whatsoever.

Somehow, he recognised her mood. 'All this will pass,' he said gently. 'Your life will pick up and you'll be happy again. Don't forget, half of what you're feeling is physical. You can't cure a massive fracture in a few weeks. The trauma stretches on for quite some time.'

She knew that, of course. Many patients suffered a vague feeling of illness and apathy long after their injuries had apparently healed. It just seemed odd to have to apply it to herself.

'Next Friday night?' he persisted.

'OK, I'll come,' she said, 'though I doubt I'll be much of a companion. But I don't want us to leave together from here. I don't want people seeing us together and starting to gossip.'

'That's fine. I'll pick you up at your house at about half-five. Wear some boating clothes—jeans or shorts and a T-shirt. But bring something warm for later.'

She thought about that. 'It sounds like you're taking me out for all of the evening. I thought we were only going to talk for an hour or so.'

'That's all we will talk for. The rest of the time we can putter along the canal, sit quietly and think nothing.'

'Sounds good,' she said after a while.

Steve Russell came round for tea that night. Kate had cooked a typically American meal. Jo quite enjoyed the hamburgers—so different when home-made! As they sat chatting afterwards Jo told them about her invitation to go on Ben's boat.

As ever, Kate was cautious and protective. 'You certainly need a new man in your life. But are you sure he's all right?'

'A man in my life is the last thing I need. Ben is just a friend, and that's all he's going to be.'

Kate still looked wary. 'You've met him, haven't you, Steve? What do you think?'

Steve, too, was wary—but a bit more forthcoming. 'I've only met him with Andrew Kirk, but each time I've talked to him I've found him to be all right.' He paused a minute and then said, 'We talked about a couple of my cases and he seemed to have the right…feeling for patients. They are people to him.'

Jo realised that this was praise, coming from Steve. She said, 'He's just a friend. Or he's getting to be a friend. He's not anyone close like you two are, but we're getting to know each other.'

'Has he tried to kiss you or anything more?' That was Kate, as blunt as ever in her defence of her sister.

'No, Kate,' Jo said irritably. 'I've told you, it's not that kind of relationship. I don't want that kind of relationship ever again.'

'Ever's a long time,' muttered Kate, and reached out to touch Steve's hand. Jo had to smile. Then the smile twisted. Once she had been in love like that.

On Friday, when Jo came off duty, she changed into the clothes Ben had suggested—jeans, soft shoes to protect his decks, a T-shirt and a sweater over her shoulders. He called for her promptly at half past five. For most of the day he had been running a clinic, and was still dressed in his semi-formal medical gear— dark shoes and trousers, a pink and white striped shirt and a rather radiant scarlet tie.

He saw her looking at it. 'We have to persuade our patients that life isn't all gloom,' he said. 'I like to think that my tie contributes to the general joy in the world.'

'It certainly lights things up. D'you think I could wear a skirt in that pattern?'

He frowned at his reflection in the hall mirror. 'Perhaps not,' he said. 'A little of this material goes a long way.'

It was only a twenty-five-minute drive to the marina. As they turned into the car park of the Waterside Inn, she saw that it was quite full, and people were sitting outside in the early evening sun. 'Quite a lot of people come here,' he told her, 'but I thought we'd go to a quieter, smaller place a couple of miles up the canal.'

'Whatever you want.' She sat in the cockpit as he went below to change, happy just to be there, to smell bacon cooking in a narrow boat close by, to hear the ducks quacking on the water. It was peaceful.

Then he came back, dressed as she was in jeans and T-shirt. It was the first time she had seen him dressed that way and he looked good, lean and muscled with no trace of fat. 'Let's go,' he said.

He pulled up a hatch in the companionway, pulled and pushed assorted things, and two minutes later there was a series of thumps, then a shudder and a burbling sound. She could hear water being discharged into the canal.

'Run up forward and cast off,' he said. 'That means untie the rope and throw it onto the foredeck.'

'Aye, aye, sir. I could have worked that out for myself.' She did as she was told.

The narrow boats seemed to be packed as tightly as sardines and she wondered whether he would hit anything as his boat slowly headed out of its narrow slot. She ran back to the cockpit and jumped aboard. She thought they would never get round the corner and into the canal. But suddenly there was a different noise, and the narrow boat's bows swung into the gap. He smiled at her surprise. 'There's a special little propeller at the front,' he said. 'Makes manoeuvring so much easier.' And they headed into the canal.

'You've done this before,' she said. 'You're an expert.'

'It's just like moving the *Queen Elizabeth*. The thing to remember is never to do anything in a hurry. If you switch the engine off, the narrow boat will carry on moving for another five minutes.'

They set off down the canal. At first there were a few narrow boats moored by the bank, but soon they were left behind and theirs was the only craft on the smooth water. On one side was the tow path, with the occasional jogger or man exercising his dog. But otherwise the evening was theirs alone.

Jo had never experienced anything quite like it. Four miles an hour was quite fast enough. They were moving but there was no sense of speed or urgency. There was time to look round, to enjoy the scenery. She spotted a heron with its clumsy, splashing take-off and its elegant flight. After a while another narrow boat came towards them, and they exchanged waves in a casual fashion.

'Your turn to steer,' he said after a while. 'I've gone more than two hours without a cup of tea.'

She looked at him in horror. 'I can't steer this! Look at the length of it!'

'Just have confidence. Remember that everything takes a long time, so you start turning well before you think it's necessary. Here, hold the tiller and try to steer towards that bank of reeds. A nice long curve. But do it slowly.'

Ben took her hand under his and showed her how even a little movement would have a large effect—after a while. Then he removed his hand and watched as she took the narrow boat in a graceful curve round a bend in the canal. 'You're a natural,' he said. 'I'll leave it to you.'

'You can't do that! Look, there's another narrow boat coming towards us!'

'Then you can steer past it. Practise keeping to this bank, and always look well ahead. Look beyond the narrow boat, see where you're steering to.'

It was surprisingly easy to follow his relaxed instructions. Jo passed the oncoming narrow boat—even managing a little wave—and then felt much more competent. 'You can go and make the tea now,' she told him. 'If there's any emergency, I'll scream.'

But she knew she wouldn't have to scream. She could do this and she was enjoying it. When he disappeared down the companionway she was quite happy.

They sat and drank tea together. It was so pleasant. There was the early evening sun, the pungent smell of the water, the summer smell of the wheat fields, the warmth on her arms and neck. In the background was the chugging of the engine, and from time to time the whistle of a bird. All her senses were involved, she felt enveloped. There was nothing else to think of, nothing to worry about. For the first time in weeks she relaxed.

'Is this therapy?' she asked suddenly.

'Certainly not. It's steering a narrow boat. Just do it and enjoy it.'

So she did, and was happy.

They rounded a bend and ahead of them was a lock. She could see the great wooden gates, dimly hear the rushing of water. 'What do we do now?' she asked.

'Well, we've just been passed by a narrow boat so we can motor straight in.' He stooped and handed her a large metal object, like an old car's starting handle. 'This is a lock key. You're going to open the far doors.'

'But I don't know how...'

'I'll tell you,' he said soothingly. 'Now, get ready to scramble ashore.' Ben took the tiller from her, and throttled back the engine. When they were nearly at the lock he steered close to the bank, and she jumped onto the tow-path, clutching the lock key. Following his instructions, she ran up to the side of the lock. The narrow boat slowly nosed in below her. it seemed odd to look down on him, with the water splashing down from the closed lock gates.

'Now get to the end of that big beam and push,' he shouted.

Jo did as she was told. Slowly, one massive lock gate swung across behind the narrow boat. 'Now go across the little bridge and push the other to meet it.'

She did. The narrow boat was enclosed in a dank, black, water-sprayed box.

'Go to the other set of gates. See that machine with the big cog wheel? Well, push the lock key into it and wind upwards.'

Once again she did as she was told. There was a rattle, a creak of machinery, but it was soon easier than she had imagined. Behind her there was the roar of water. She looked down at the narrow boat again. To one side of it water was boiling upwards, pushing the narrow boat against the lock wall. 'Go and do the same on the other side.'

Again, she did. And there was more water rushing into the lock. When she looked the water level in the lock was much higher and the narrow boat was being gently lifted upwards.

Finally, the water in the lock was level with the water in the next stretch of canal. She opened two more gates—and the narrow boat drifted out.

She ran along the tow-path, and jumped back aboard. 'Easy, wasn't it?' he asked.

'Piece of cake,' she told him. It had been a simple, physical task. But she had found it tremendously satisfying.

They sailed on for another half hour until they came to another lock, but this one had a pub by it. There was also what seemed to be a large basin—Ben called it a winding circle. 'We'll turn round here,' he said. 'Then we'll moor and go to the pub for some supper. Are you hungry?'

She hadn't been hungry for weeks—most of the time she just picked at her food. Her weight had gone down. 'I'm ravenous,' she said.

They walked to the pub—one of the many called the Navigation Inn—and had a simple meal, sitting outside. Then they walked back to the narrow boat and set off for home. After twenty minutes Ben cut the engine. The narrow boat drifted to a stop and he jumped ashore and moored it. They were alone. To each side were great corn fields. There was no one, no building nearby. Only the canal stretching in front of them, now dancing with the gold of the setting sun.

At first, when the engine stopped, Jo thought that everything was silent. But then she heard the almost imperceptible sounds of the countryside, the rustle of animals in the wheat, the far-off cry of birds. It lulled her.

She knew why he had stopped. 'You want me to talk now, don't you?' she asked.

Ben shrugged. 'I want you to sit here and enjoy the peace of the evening,' he said. 'If you want to talk, then what better time or place? But only if you want to.'

'I don't *want* to talk. But perhaps I ought to. What should I talk about?'

He thought for a minute. 'You've told me how you first met Harry. Tell me how you felt when Steve came through that door and told you that the wedding was off. I know this must be the worst memory of your life, and you don't want to relive it. But...it might help. This is what you've got to face and come through. What were your emotions? What did you feel?'

It was hard to do. Surprisingly, when she tried to concentrate on what had happened, her mind swerved away. She realised she had built a wall round what had happened, the details escaped her. But she forced herself, and dragged the memories back from where they had been hiding.

First she had been so happy—her twin sister had come home. Then the unsmiling Steve had appeared at the door. She just hadn't been able to comprehend what he'd been saying. There had been that jumble of feelings—disbelief, horror, anger, self-pity. As she looked back to that time the emotions presented themselves again and she was torn apart now as she had been then. The tears welled.

'How could he?' she sobbed. 'I loved him. Why didn't he give me some idea? We could have worked something out...postponed it if he wanted. But just to go. And not to tell me to my face—just one short letter. Here, I'll show you, just one short letter. This is all the feeling he had left for me, just one short letter!' And from the purse in her pocket she wrenched a flimsy sheet of paper, thrust it towards Ben.

He took it, read it.

Ben looked bleak. 'Why are you keeping this?' he asked. 'Do you keep it with you always, move it when you change clothes?'

'Yes, I do! I do it so I can remember what a rat he is.'

'Doesn't it make you angry, keeping it with you always? Aren't you always aware that it's there? Shouldn't you stop thinking of him and just think of you?'

'Are you saying I ought to throw it away? This is the proof of what a louse he is.'

'Why d'you need proof? It looks much read, surely you know what it says by now?'

'So I should throw it away?'

'Only if you want to. Only if you think you'll be happier with it gone. Only if you'll never regret getting rid of it. What does keeping it do for you? Or do to you?'

There was silence for a minute. Then Jo said, 'All you do is ask questions. You don't give me advice.'

'I'm not going to give you advice. All I can do is listen.'

For a moment she stared at the scrap of paper, then slowly, deliberately, tore it into tiny pieces. She held them in the palm of her hand, and looked at the canal. 'I'll not be a litter lout,' she said, with the tiniest of smiles.

Silently he went down the companionway, returned with a large ashtray and a box of matches. He placed them in front of her. Making sure that not one scrap escaped, she dropped the fragments of paper into the ashtray and set fire to them. When they were all consumed, she tipped the blackened ash over the side.

'How d'you feel?' he asked.

'Better—but tired.'

He offered her his handkerchief and she wiped her face with it. 'Being on the narrow boat calms me,' she said. 'You're a very clever man.' She slid beside him. When he put his arm round her shoulders she rested her head on him. He was comforting. She found herself dropping off to sleep.

Jo slept for perhaps ten minutes. At the end of that time she woke, feeling still tired but somehow serene. 'Your arm must be hurting,' she said.

'No problem, you're no weight at all. But it gets dark in an hour. Perhaps we should set off back.'

'I'll go to your bathroom,' she said. 'I feel a wreck.'

She looked a wreck, too. But after washing her face and making a few repairs, she decided that things could be worse. She went back to the cockpit to find that Ben had cast off and they were moving once more. 'Can I steer again?' she asked.

'Of course. You're becoming an expert.'

After ten minutes' companionable silence she said, 'I thought that never again would I go to sleep leaning on a man's chest.'

'All part of the service,' Ben said comfortably.

CHAPTER FOUR

'YOU and Steve are going to the hospital summer picnic, aren't you?' Jo asked Kate.

It was Monday, ten days later, and the two of them were having breakfast before driving into work. Jo had her head bowed, pretending to be concentrating on her grapefruit, but was aware of Kate looking at her carefully.

'We might,' Kate said, elaborately casual, 'but we're not very keen.'

'Rubbish. I know you can both get the time off. The only reason you're thinking of not going is because of me.' Jo was determined to be firm. 'I'm all right. Go and enjoy yourselves.'

'We don't like to think of you sitting here being miserable while we go out,' said Kate. 'And I remember…you…'

'That's the past, it doesn't matter,' said Jo. 'I know Steve would like to go, so you two go together.'

'We'll think about it,' said Kate.

The hospital summer picnic was one of the two most important events organised by the hospital welfare committee. Really, it marked the end of summer. Sir Michael Gilmore, a local industrialist, let them take over the grounds of Gilmore Hall for the day. There would be a big marquee for dancing, fairy-lights in the grounds, a great barbecue. Everyone always enjoyed it.

Jo thought about last year. It had been like a fairy-land indeed. The weather had been wonderful, she'd danced all night, it had been so warm in the darkness afterwards... Tears threatened to squeeze through, but fortunately Kate didn't notice.

'I shall be annoyed if you and Steve don't go,' Jo said.

Jo hadn't seen Ben for over a week. He'd been sent to a neighbouring hospital because one of the surgeons there had been taken ill. Now Andrew had gone for a few days and Ben was back by her side, clad in greens, scrubbing up.

She had missed him. But he had phoned a couple of times, casual calls in the evenings, just to catch up on the gossip, he had said. It felt good to have him with her again. It seemed longer than ten days since their trip on the narrow boat.

'People have been telling me about this summer pic-nic,' he said casually. 'Are you going to go?'

'No,' she said flatly.

He carried on scrubbing his nails. 'That was very definitely said.'

After a pause she said, 'On the evening of last year's picnic Harry asked me to marry him and I walked round showing everybody his grandmother's engagement ring which he had given me. I was walking on air. I can't ever remember being as happy as I was that day.'

'So will you stay at home and mope?'

'No, I guess I'll work in the garden and be quite happy.' She thought for a moment and then said honestly, 'I guess that means that I'll mope.'

'Are Kate and Steve going?'

'I'll be angry if they don't go because of me. I hope they do.' The words stuck in her throat because she loved her sister and Steve but she managed to say, 'This year she can show everyone *her* engagement ring.'

'We've all seen it,' Ben said happily. 'Nothing new there. Now, I've got a confession. I phoned Steve this morning and asked him if I could join his party. I'd like us to go as a foursome. He said he was delighted and knew Kate would be, too.'

'You did what? You want me to go as your partner? You didn't think about asking me first, I suppose?'

'Well, I want us to go as friends rather than partners. I know you've kept out of the social round recently, and I thought this was a good chance for you to get back into it.'

'But people there will remember me flashing my ring!'

'So this time flash your ringless finger. You're starting again, Jo. Never mind what's past. Think about the future.'

'But why d'you want to take me? There's plenty of young nurses who—'

'We're pals, Jo. We're part of the team, we get on well together. I expect we'll spend a lot of time sitting with Andrew and his family. You'll enjoy it. Now, tell me about this operation we've got coming up…'

'Are you sure he doesn't fancy you?' asked Kate that night.

Jo laughed. 'It's not that kind of relationship at all. Like they say, we're just good friends. I just think I ought to go to this—show my face, not mope at home. I'm fighting back.'

'That's the spirit,' Kate said approvingly. 'And Steve likes Ben no end. He phoned him up a couple of days ago. Apparently Steve had a kid in, thought there was a slight chance he might have meningitis. He didn't want to refer him at once so he got in touch with Ben for a bit of unofficial advice. Ben couldn't have been more helpful. The two of them will get on together. Can Ben dance?'

Something caught at Jo's throat. Harry had been a great dancer. Perhaps he was a bit flashy, he loved intricate steps, but he could lead like an angel. 'I don't anticipate doing much dancing,' she said.

'I bet you change your mind. Now, what are you going to wear?'

Jo was willing to be persuaded to go to the picnic, but no way could she work up much enthusiasm for it. Certainly, she wasn't going to buy anything new. 'There'll be something in my wardrobe,' she said.

'Well, thank you for that outburst of excitement. No, Jo, at a do like his, a girl is what she wears. If you look good you feel good. Now, come along to my bedroom. I've got all my stuff back from Vegas now and some of it you haven't yet seen.'

Kate rummaged through her wardrobe. 'Not formal,' she said, 'but something that shows that you know you're somebody. How about this? Yes, this is perfect!'

Jo looked at it dubiously. 'It'll be all right if it keeps warm,' she said.

The dress couldn't have been simpler, a clinging

white silk confection to just below knee level sleeveless and with a fitted top. Jo tried it on.

'That's it, no question,' said Kate. 'You look marvellous. You'll have to buy some of that no-show
underwear and you'll look absolutely stunning.'

'All right,' said Jo.

'I'm not going to drink,' Jo said to Ben two days before the picnic. 'It hasn't brought me much pleasure
lately. So I'll drive. Kate and I will pick up you and
Steve.'

Ben looked surprised at this. 'I don't drink a vast
amount myself,' he said, 'but I thought we might have
a taxi for the evening.'

'There won't be enough local taxis to go round,' Jo
said, 'and I want to do this. You don't mind, do you?'

'No,' said Ben after a moment. 'If you don't mind
I think it's a very good idea.'

Jo didn't spend as much time as Kate getting ready
for the party when the day arrived. At one moment
she felt that sick feeling that the whole affair was
pointless. For most people this picnic—to be frank—
was the chance to show off their sexual partner. A
husband, a fiancé, a boyfriend. She had none of these,
just a good friend. They might just as well have stayed
at home and watched television. Then she heard Kate
singing happily in the bath, and decided she *would* be
happy.

She had the traditional long luxurious bath, set her
hair, borrowed some of Kate's expensive perfume.
Then the two of them stood in the hall, admiring each
other.

'Gorgeous, the pair of us,' Kate said. She was wearing a dark blue dress that emphasised the tan she still had from America. 'Come on. Let's go and pick up these two men.' Jo hid a smile. Kate was obviously going to enjoy herself.

They collected Steve and Ben. 'You two men can sit together in the back,' said Kate. Then they drove to Gilmore Hall. There was a large field designated for parking, and a line of people walking towards the marquee.

The picnic was supposed to be a casual event—as opposed to the more formal Christmas party. But most people had spent quite a bit of money trying to look casual. So many of the people Jo knew in hospital spent their time in scrubs or uniform that it was quite interesting to see what they chose to wear as civvies. She got more than a few surprises.

They handed in their tickets and accepted a complimentary drink of champagne or orange juice. Then they walked through the trees towards the sound of music. Steve was talking to Ben for a moment and Kate pulled her sister to one side. 'Listen, and I mean this, if you can't cope then we're both going home. I might be here to enjoy myself, but I'll be watching you.'

'I can cope,' said Jo, 'and I'm going to enjoy myself—even if it kills me.'

Kate squeezed her. 'That's my sister. Don't let them grind you down.'

Jo grinned. Her sister was good at saying the right things.

They were lucky with the weather. It was getting towards the end of summer, but the air was fresh and balmy. Now in couples, they walked towards the marquee, the sound of the band getting louder. Kate and Steve were ahead, laughing at some private joke.

It happened less often these days, but suddenly there was that flash of memory of times when things had been so different. Jo remembered being here on Harry's arm. She had been so excited, so happy. The realisation that he had gone from her life hit her again, like a blow. She stopped, swayed slightly.

Someone—it had to be Ben—took her arm and folded it over his. 'There's a forfeit to coming here with me,' he said calmly. 'I'm afraid you have to dance with me. Not something to look forward to. But I'm sure you'll be a brave girl and suffer with fortitude.'

The nonsensical words were just what she needed. She turned to him with a strained smile and said, 'I promise to be brave. But remember, you're dancing with a girl with a recently broken leg.' He squeezed her arm again and they walked on in silence.

After a while she asked curiously, 'How did you know to say that just then? How did you know that I needed comforting?'

'I wasn't comforting you, I was warning you,' he said lazily. 'Anything else was pure chance.'

'Ben Franklin! I don't believe you.'

They reached the top of a little rise and below them was a hollow. The marquee was at one end. Its sides had been roped up, a wooden floor laid for dancing and a band played just outside. There were formal gardens in the rest of the hollow, and tables with candles on them were scattered throughout. There was a bar, a barbecue and a stall selling other food. It all looked magical.

'Andrew and his family are here somewhere,' said Ben. 'Shall we try to find them?'

Just as he spoke there was a shout, and there was Andrew waving at them. There were plenty of seats so they sat to talk a while. Andrew was there with his wife Penny and his two little girls, Jen and Jan. Jo liked the family. They had been good friends to her. And she thought it a lovely idea that young children could come to a party with their parents.

It was an amiable, casual evening. People wandered to their table, sat to chat a while and then wandered off. Jo didn't really want to walk too much, her leg could still pain her at times.

After a while Jo found herself sitting alone at the table with Jen and Jan, both of whom were noisily sucking lemonade through fancy straws. Andrew and Penny and Steve and Kate were dancing. Then Ben came and sat by her, having fetched a tray of drinks.

As she sipped her iced orange Jo felt at ease, calmer than she had done for a while. For the past few weeks she had avoided big crowds, preferring to work and to worry over her problems at home. But now she was actually enjoying herself. She wondered if that flash of horror over Harry which she had experienced earlier would be the last. She knew she was getting better. And it was largely due to Ben. He'd been a pal. Talking to him had helped so much.

With a loud rattle Jen, the older girl, finished her lemonade. Then she looked reproachfully at Jo.

'You didn't get married,' she said. 'And I wanted to be a bridesmaid, we both did. And we've still got the dresses and we try them on when Mummy lets us.'

Jo felt Ben's hand, warm and comforting on the bare skin of her back. It was gentle, encouraging.

'I'm sorry,' she said, 'but Harry and I decided not to get married.'

'Why not? I've never been to a wedding.'

Fortunately, Jo didn't seem to be expected to answer the question.

Ben passed Jen another bottle of lemonade, but the little girl wasn't to be deflected. 'I want you to get married then we can wear our dresses. Why can't you marry Ben? You're not married, are you, Ben? Wouldn't you like to marry Jo?'

'I'd love to marry Jo,' came the calm reply, 'but your daddy would never forgive me if I took Jo away from him. He needs her in his work and I do, too. We're a good team, aren't we, Jo?'

Jo replied equally calmly, 'Yes. We're a good team.' She was surprised at how she felt, neither upset nor irritated. This was only a little girl and she didn't understand.

Andrew and Penny came back from dancing. As they sat down Jen said, 'Daddy, let Ben marry Jo and then we can wear our bridesmaids' outfits. Ben says it's your fault they can't get married.'

Jo saw Penny grow pale, and even Andrew winced. Quickly she said, 'I'd forgotten that you were going to be bridesmaids, but I know you looked very nice. But I promise that when I do get married you can be my bridesmaids. All right?'

But now Jen was more interested in her new lemonade. She took a great mouthful, then lifted her head. 'Mind you don't forget,' she said.

'I think it's time you paid your forfeit,' said Ben.

'You have to dance with me now. This seems to be a slow one.'

The band was alternating with a disco, and was about to play a waltz. Jo walked over with Ben and joined the slowly swaying crowd. He was, in fact, quite a good dancer. As in everything he did, he was dependable, steady.

'You coped very well there,' he said after a while. 'I'd forgotten how appallingly honest children could be.'

'I'm not made of glass. I'll survive—in fact, I think I'm better already.' They circled the floor again. 'Oh, and thanks for the proposal of marriage—I suppose it was a proposal?'

'My pleasure,' he said urbanely.

On Monday morning she and Ben were summoned to Andrew's office.

'I think this is good news,' Andrew said. 'I've checked your schedules, and you're both free next weekend. Is there anything personal that you just can't get out of?'

Both shook their heads.

'You're lucky. I've got a day-long meeting in London I just can't get out of.' He took up a thick envelope from his desk. 'This is something I was very interested in. Reardon Medical Supplies—you know, the American firm—has just developed a set of new instruments and techniques for using cryogenics in brain surgery.' He sifted through the papers in the envelope. 'There's a lot of good evidence here to suggest that this could be a real breakthrough.'

'I read about it in a journal last month,' Ben said

eagerly. 'It was fascinating stuff. Would help no end in some of our operations.'

Jo had only had a little experience of cryogenics. She knew that it involved using a probe that was super-cooled. It excised warts, and in eye surgery welded detached retinas. 'How could it be used in neurosurgery?' she asked.

Andrew frowned. 'Well, I know it's been used occasionally to remove single lesions from the brain—a cyst or an isolated cerebral tumour. But that's about all. However, Reardon's think that it could be used an awful lot more.'

He pushed a coloured pamphlet across the desk towards Jo and Ben. 'They've organised a weekend seminar to demonstrate and teach the new techniques. Numbers are strictly limited. I did apply but we were too late. Now I've just been told that there's been a cancellation, so if we want to we can send a theatre nurse and a surgeon. It starts this coming Friday. Do you two want to go?'

'Yes,' both said without hesitation.

'Good. I'll fax confirmation at once. It should be enjoyable, though intensive. You can both report back to me next Monday morning and we'll decide if we want any of this new equipment out of this year's budget.'

'How d'you feel about going?' Ben asked when they were out of Andrew's room.

'Great. If I can get in at the beginning of something new, then it can only help my career.'

'Good. Would you like to travel up with me? We can have another chat about Harry if you want.'

'I'd love to travel up with you. But no need to worry

about Harry. I feel he's nearly behind me. You've helped me get him in perspective. Now I can worry about the rest of my life—and cryogenics looks like a good start.'

The joining instructions for the weekend course were waiting for her when she got home next evening, and she read them with interest. There was a short introduction to cryogenics. Apparently super-cooled liquid nitrogen was pumped down a probe and used to kill off malignant cells. Then the gaseous nitrogen was sucked back up another section of the probe. The great advantage was that there was minimal invasion of the surrounding tissue—no need to cut away to reveal what was malignant. The big problem, however, was monitoring just how much tissue was affected by the super-cooling. Jo realised at once just how useful the technique could be. Quite often the surgeons had to work in incredibly constricted conditions in the skull.

'So you're going on a little holiday with Ben?' Kate asked cheerfully. 'Where exactly are you going?'

'Not really a holiday, I'm going to work. I intend to learn something.' Jo leafed through the documents spread out in front of her. 'Apparently we're meeting in a big hotel, somewhere on the banks of Lake Coniston.' She passed a photograph to her sister. 'That's the place.'

'Looks lovely,' said Kate. 'Who knows what might happen in a romantic setting like that?'

'Nothing will happen. They're going to work us too hard for that.'

Jo took a case into work on Friday, and when work was over changed out of her scrubs into smart dark trousers and a blue silk shirt. Ben was also dressed casually but smartly. They climbed into his little car and set off for the motorway north.

'I've never been to a residential course like this,' she told him. 'I don't know what to expect.'

'You often learn a lot. Just chatting to other people in the same line of business can be very instructive. You'll be very popular.'

'Why?' she asked curiously.

'Because there will be more men there than women—and you're a very attractive woman.'

'I'm off men,' she reminded him, 'but, still, thanks for the compliment.'

'It doesn't matter if you're off men. They can still dream.'

The motorway was quite crowded. Even though it had been grey all day, it was still summer and there were many other cars heading for the Lakes.

After a while Ben said, 'I think you're a lot more confident now. Not angry any more, happier in yourself, you don't have doubts about your worth. If I say Harry Russell to you, you don't automatically flinch. You can look back and it makes you sad, but you now know that the sadness wasn't in the least caused by you. You are blameless. Is that right?'

'Yes,' Jo said after a moment. 'There is the odd twinge, of course—after all, he was the centre of my life for over a year, something must be missing. But I'm putting something back in its place. I'm me, I'm good at my job, I'm highly regarded by people whose opinion I value. And most of all I'm loved by my friends and family.'

'That's good. Do you think—will you ever—could you fall in love again?'

'That would be going too far.'

When they could see the distant peaks of the Lake District on the horizon, the first drops of rain tapped on the windscreen. Five minutes later the rain increased, and by the time they were skirting the foothills they were in a steady downpour.

'I've brought my walking boots,' Ben said mournfully, 'but if it's going to be like this all weekend I don't see much chance of using them. This is typical Lakes weather.'

'Lakes weather can change.'

In spite of the rain they made good time and soon she was map-reading through a maze of small roads to take them to the east bank of Lake Coniston, the quieter side.

Ferry Park Hotel was an old converted house. The grounds were full of rhododendrons and the lawns ran down to the water's edge where there was a jetty and a few rowing boats upside down. The building itself was in traditional grey stone with a slate roof. An obviously new wing had been tastefully added to one side. And all of it was made colourless by the rain.

They parked, grabbed their cases and ran for the foyer. The hall itself was very pleasant, panelled in oak and with a rich red carpet. A smiling receptionist gave them each a room key and a large folder and suggested they might like to meet in half an hour for a pre-dinner drink in the library.

'Shall we dress for dinner?' Ben asked Jo.

'I think we'd better try to look nice. Not exactly

evening dress, but I think everyone else will be making an effort.'

'Let me carry your case to your room.'

'It's OK I can manage.'

'All right. Shall I meet you in here in the hall in half an hour? Then we can go in together.'

'There's no need,' she said with a touch of annoyance. 'I can find my own way to the library. I'll see you there somewhere.'

He smiled. 'You're coming on, aren't you?'

Her room was number 137 in the new wing and she liked it at once. It was well designed, there were fresh flowers on the dressing-table and a selection of books by the bed. The bed was a double.

She showered and then looked for something suitable to wear. She had thought it might be semi-formal, and had brought a couple of long skirts which she could match with blouses.

When she was dressed and had put on her make-up, she found she still had time to leaf through the folder she had been given. It was going to be a hectic programme. There were lectures, demonstrations and workshops from nine till seven the next day and from nine till one on Sunday. Well, she had come here to work. She became fascinated by the details given of the new surgical technique, and wondered how Ben and Andrew might use it.

Then, conscious of looking well in her long grey skirt and light blue blouse, she pinned on the name badge she had been given and went downstairs. The library opened off the hall, and she could hear the mumble of conversation before she got there. She passed a few people, mostly men, mostly slightly older than her. All were formally dressed. Some gave her a covert glance—of admiration, she hoped. She must be improving in her attitude, she thought, she rather liked it.

There were about sixty people in the library, standing talking in little groups. Jo accepted a glass of red wine as she entered. She had decided that this weekend she would drink—in moderation, of course.

She looked round. Ben was already there, dressed in the traditional dark suit, white shirt and college tie that sat so well on him. He looked every inch the urbane professional. Obviously looking for her, he raised a hand and gestured for her to join him and his group.

He introduced her as 'Jo Wilde, Theatre Sister, my second pair of hands. Jo, Professor Nettley here is just telling us about some new developments in anaesthesia.' After that, she just listened, absorbed. She noticed that Ben did the same.

After half an hour they were told that dinner was served. There were no set places so she sat next to Ben. However, they said little to each other. On his other side was one of the few other women there. Her badge said that she was Eleanor Myers, a surgeon from a London hospital. Jo knew that to get to the top of this field a woman had to be determined. And Eleanor Myers was determined. Thin, in her midforties, with expensively cut hair and an equally expensive purple dress, Eleanor was going to talk to Ben, and no one was going to hinder her. Jo noticed that she had no wedding ring—and then wondered why she had noticed.

To Jo's right was a very pleasant white-haired

American. He shook hands and introduced himself as Professor Anthony Douglas.

'We're going to talk shop non-stop all tomorrow,' he said, 'so I propose to talk about something else tonight. D'you know anything about the local history of this area, Jo? I'm afraid it's a hobby of mine.'

'Just a little bit,' Jo said cautiously.

'I've noticed that a lot of the local places are called "park". There's this place, Water Park, Oxen Park, Lawson Park. I wondered why.'

'I'm afraid I have no idea,' she said.

'This is a fascinating place. My ancestors came from round here. Did you know that...' He talked about Romans and Vikings, about miners and charcoal burners, about monks and poets. As ever, Jo was impressed that a foreigner should know so much about what was her country.

The meal was superb. She had a glass of white wine with her fish and decided to have no more. At the end of the meal there was a welcome and a short introduction—given, to her surprise, by Professor Douglas, the man to her right. Then they were all invited to have coffee in the library.

'Hospital, car, hotel,' Ben whispered to her. 'I've been penned up too long. Look, it's stopped raining. D'you fancy a short walk round the grounds for a while? There are lots of gravel paths, you won't get muddy.'

'Yes, I'd like a walk.'

'Then let's go, before my friend Eleanor comes back. D'you need to fetch a coat or anything?'

'I don't think so.' Jo giggled. 'Why d'you want to

escape Eleanor?' Feeling like truants from school, the two of them made for the front door.

'I've never been offered a job with more force,' Ben said. 'Eleanor feels that we would make a great team.'

'Might do your career a lot of good.'

'No, thanks. Working with Dr Eleanor Myers would be like being tied to a steamroller. She's already explained where I've been wrong on a couple of things.'

It was now dusk, and lights in the hotel behind them made the building seem even darker. Their feet crunched as they walked the gravel path down to the lake. They rounded a shrubbery and the house was out of sight.

An odd drop of rain still pattered from a tree, but that was all. The air felt clear, smelt good. In the distance was the dark line of Coniston Old Man with a sprinkling of lights showing where the village was and the odd solitary farmhouse on the fells. In front of them was the dark silver of the Lake. The sky was still black—there was more rain to come—but they could see enough.

A small breeze rippled across the lake, the sudden chill made Jo shiver. Without speaking, Ben took off his jacket and wrapped it round her shoulders. She pulled it close. She felt warm now and the jacket smelt of him. 'You'll be cold now,' she reproached him.

'No, I'm fine.' He put his arm round her shoulders. 'I should have let you fetch a jacket or something. Isn't this wonderful? Now you know why I love water—even if it's just the muddy brown of the canal.'

'Yes, I can see. It makes you feel…peaceful.'

'Peaceful?' Ben said the word thoughtfully. 'Are you feeling more at peace in yourself now?'

'Yes, I think I am. Very much so. I'm going to focus on being even more successful in my career, and a lot of that is due to you. In fact I—'

The breeze was suddenly stronger, colder, the rattling of water falling from the trees easier to hear. And a raindrop spattered on her cheek. 'Let's go,' she said. 'In a couple of moments we're going to be drenched.'

The distant lights were now blurred, opaque, because of the squall moving across the lake. Hand in hand they rushed back to the hotel.

When they got there they decided it wasn't too late for coffee. Jo slipped to the ladies' to check on her appearance. When she came out she saw that Ben had been grabbed again, and he was already part of a small group arguing fiercely about something. Eleanor was there, too, but Ben appeared to be enjoying himself so she didn't try to rescue him.

She took a cup of coffee. Professor Douglas was standing by the table, deep in conversation with a small sunburned man in a black suit. 'Ah, Jo! This is Mr Rawson—he's the manager here and an expert on local history. He can answer my question about why there are so many parks. Apparently they were outlying sheep farms set up by the monks of Furness Abbey.'

She didn't have to spend all her time up here with Ben. Mr Rawson and the Professor were a pair of fascinating companions and she thoroughly enjoyed talking—or to be more exact, listening—to them. But she kept looking across at Ben.

Eventually she found herself yawning, and Professor Douglas chuckled and said that was a sure indication that they'd talked enough. He and Mr

Rawson said goodnight, but she noticed that they walked off to the manager's office. Others there had had an even longer journey, and people started to drift off to bed. She saw Ben's little group breaking up and went across.

'I've really enjoyed myself but I'm tired and I'm going to bed,' she said to him. 'Did you have a good evening?'

'I enjoyed the evening but I missed you. See you in the morning?' They were now in the hall. He bent over and kissed her on the cheek.

'See you in the morning,' she said, and suddenly thought that it was the first time that he had kissed her.

Jo ran a bath when she got to her room, then put on the little kettle and shook a packet of cocoa into a mug. She was tired but she knew she wouldn't sleep at once. After hanging up her clothes, she climbed into the bath with her drink. She had to think.

Twice today she had said it—she was free of the memory of Harry. And it was true. When she thought of him she didn't automatically feel hurt or angry. She could even remember some of the good times they had had together. That part of her life was now over—she could look to the future. Of course she had learned, she wouldn't fall into the same trap again. She wouldn't give all of herself, concentrate all her thoughts, her hopes, her future, on one man. Now she was her own person. She felt a small glow of satisfaction.

She climbed out of the bath, wrapped herself in one of the large towels and sat on the bed. Life had a lot to offer her. Starting now.

CHAPTER FIVE

SATURDAY was hard. They started with a lecture and a film, and then there was a demonstration given to the entire group. For the rest of the weekend they were to work in smaller groups, and as a theatre nurse rather than a surgeon, Jo was in a different group from Ben.

Yes, the work was hard. But as she went through the day, Jo was shown what the new technique could do and was asked how it could have affected operations she had taken part in in the past—she realised it could be of great use. She hoped Andrew and Ben would decide to buy the equipment. Much of the responsibility for operating it would be hers, but she felt this was something she could deal with.

There was short break for a buffet lunch, during which she managed to have a quick word with Ben. 'I'm enjoying it but I'm longing for some fresh air,' he said. 'Have you seen what it's like outside?'

Well, no, she'd hardly noticed. But the rain had gone and in the sunshine, the colours on the far fellside were beautiful. 'We're here to work,' she told him with a smile. 'Just concentrate on that.'

The afternoon was just as fascinating and just as hard. This time they were allowed to use the instruments and were shown the techniques of handling them. By the time the last session finished she thought she had never worked a harder day.

Ben felt the same. When they met for a pre-dinner

drink he whispered to her, 'I just can't stand another evening talking in the library. It might be doing my career some good but a man needs a rest. After dinner we'll sneak off to our rooms, change into something more comfortable and walk along the road a bit. That suit you?'

'Sounds wonderful,' she told him, feeling pleasantly wicked. 'Today's been good but stressful. Are we sitting together at dinner again?'

But somehow, when they went into dinner, Eleanor Myers was sitting on the other side of Ben. And after dinner he was escorted into the library, whether he wanted to go or not. He caught Jo's eye, winked and shrugged. Jo winked back and pointed upstairs. She would go and change.

It was an hour before he managed to escape. There was a tap on her door, and he slid quickly in as she opened it. 'The trouble is,' he said, 'what she says is quite interesting and quite useful. But I've had it with learning today. I want out. D'you still want a walk?'

She had changed into jeans and a sweater, and had put on heavy shoes. 'Of course I do,' she said. She pointed to the window. 'But it's dark now. Do you still want to go?'

He was still in his formal suit. 'You bet I do. Give me five minutes to change and I'll see you outside the front door.'

It was warm and calm. The sky was clear, and it was easy to see by starlight. When Ben appeared he was carrying what seemed to be two long poles over his shoulder. 'Oars,' he said. 'I borrowed them from the manager.'

'Oars?'

'I fancied a change from walking. Come on.'

He led her to where they had seen the rowing boats turned upside down on the little beach. They turned one over, slid it into the water and pulled it to the jetty. Then he helped her down into it, fitted the rowlocks and oars and pushed off. 'This is wonderful,' she said. 'I've never been out on a lake in the dark before.'

Ben was obviously used to rowing, pulling easily into the centre of the lake. She turned to look over her shoulder. The lakeside behind her seemed to slip away, the sounds of conversation grew less. It was so peaceful. There seemed to be no need to talk. The lake spread out around them, still and dark. The silence was now total. There was only the creak of the rowlocks and the drip of the water falling from the oars. He seemed as affected as she was. They were together, at peace.

She looked at the long line of the fells, an infrequent light seeming to make them look even more lonely. There was now the occasional sound of a car on the road, a faint burst of laughter from somewhere. All she could see of Ben was a silhouette, the broadness of his shoulders, perhaps the paleness of his face. She was happy to be with him.

'You're not too cold?' he whispered.

'No, I feel warm here with you.' She dipped her hand over the side, felt the chill of the water. 'But the lake is very cold. I suppose it's because of the rain.'

'Lake Coniston is always cold. It's very deep. There are hundreds of feet of water under us right now.'

She shivered at the thought. He stopped rowing and they sat there, surrounded by the immensity of lake and mountain. It seemed to wrap round them, holding them in the centre of darkness.

She was glad to be out here with him, wanted to be closer to him. But she knew better than to try and move in a rowing boat, the flimsy craft were so easy to capsize. She pushed off one of her shoes, reached out her foot and stroked his leg with it. He said nothing. But she knew it pleased him.

'I'm glad you brought me out here,' she said after a while. 'I'm enjoying it so much. But perhaps it's time we were going back. We have to move on.'

'Yes, we always have to move on.'

He seemed to row back more quickly. The stem of the boat crunched into the shingle, he jumped out, pulled the boat ashore, helped her out. Then he turned the boat over, picked up the oars.

Jo stood motionless in the dark. She didn't want to move yet. There was something she had to do—or something that had to be done. Ben looked at her and then put down the oars.

His body was silhouetted against the starlight. She saw him move, then hesitate, as if unsure. Then he dropped the oars, stepped forward and took her in his arms.

For a second she hesitated. Then she stretched her arms round him and pulled him to her.

His kiss at first was tentative, gentle, but she now knew that she wanted more. She moved hard against him. His hand caressed the back of her head, holding her to him. This was so good! There was darkness all round them, but she felt as if she had just moved into the sun, into the light out of the greyness of the past few weeks. She came alive again, wanting to be with this man.

Gently he disengaged himself, ignoring her plaintive whispered objections. 'I wanted to do that,' he muttered. 'I hadn't realised how much I wanted to do that. But we shouldn't, it's not right for you, not yet. I'm trying to help you and I—'

She interrupted him. 'I'm a big girl now. I know my own mind. You didn't do anything to me, we did it to each other, we did it together. And it was wonderful. What time is it?'

The prosaic question seemed to shock him. He looked at the luminous dial of his watch and in a tone of disbelief said, 'It's only ten o'clock, but such a lot seems to have happened.'

'A lot has happened,' she told him.

Behind them they could hear sounds of conversation and laughter from the hotel. 'D'you want to go inside, perhaps have a drink?' he asked her.

Her answer was prompt. 'No. I've had enough with meeting other people today. That is...well, there's a kettle in my room. D'you want to come in for tea or coffee or something?'

There was silence between them. Then he said, in an effort to lighten the tone, 'We've all got TV as well. We could sit on the bed and watch the news or something.'

'We *could* watch the news,' she said, 'though I doubt we will.'

There was silence again. 'D'you know what you're doing?' he asked.

'I know what I'm doing, I've thought about it, I'm happy about it.' She leaned up to kiss him.

He picked up the oars again and they walked to the hotel together. Outside, she let go of his hand and said, 'You know the number of my room, it's 137. Why don't you come round in about fifteen minutes? I'll have the kettle on.'

Still uncertain, he said, 'I will. If you're sure that's what you want.'

'That's what I want. See you in a quarter of an hour.'

She went to her room, feeling she was a different kind of woman, another person. She didn't want to think. Too much of her time recently had been spent thinking. Now was *not* the time to think.

Swiftly she wriggled out of her clothes and kicked them into the cupboard. She had a shower and then grinned. At home she had sheer nightgowns, but for this trip she had brought plain pink pyjamas. So what? She put them on, slipped on her dressing-gown afterwards. That was all right.

The minute she sat on her bed she could feel her heart drumming. Did she know what she was doing? She had never acted like this before. Then she decided. Yes, she knew exactly what she was doing.

She put on the kettle as she had promised, then switched off the main light and switched on the two bedside lights. She opened the curtains and looked out. It would have been nice to have had a long view of the lake or the fellside. Instead, there was only a view of the back of the house. She smiled. You couldn't have everything. Life wasn't romantic in every way. Still, she opened the window. There was the scent of woods and the good smell of the countryside.

Someone knocked at the door. For a moment she

felt panic, apprehension, but then she opened it. Ben was there. He wore dark trousers and a white shirt, having changed. In one hand were two wineglasses, in the other a bottle of wine.

Stepping inside, he said, 'I bought this downstairs. A lot of people were buying wine. It's Barolo—a light Italian white. I thought you would like something not too heavy. We can talk while drinking it.'

'I would like a glass,' she told him, 'perhaps two. But I don't want to talk too much. I'm tired of talking, and I'm especially tired of talking about myself.'

He put the glasses on the table, filled them with white wine.

'I'd like to talk about you, though,' she said. 'You know, we've never done that.'

He handed her a glass, kicked off his shoes and sat cross-legged on the bed, his own glass in his hand. Both tasted. It was good, clean and fresh-tasting, a faint prickle on the tongue. She sat in a chair, happy so far, and stretched her legs. 'Why are you called Ben Franklin?' she asked. 'Wasn't he an American hero?'

Ben nodded. 'He was a fascinating man—a scientist as well as a politician. He was the man who proved lightning was a form of electricity by flying a kite in a storm. Afterwards he helped draft the American Declaration of Independence. My mother named me Ben—I think it was a tiny revolt on her part, an attempt to establish some independence of her own. I've always been proud of the name. It's something to live up to.'

'You're not mentioning your father,' Jo said. 'Was that who your mother needed to be independent of?'

'I'll tell you about my family another time,' he said. 'Now I'm more interested in you. Or in us.'

Both fell silent. He reached out and set his empty glass down on the bedside table. The ting it made seemed loud in her bedroom. There was the distant sound of conversation but it seemed far away, nothing to do with them. From the still open window came the faintest of breezes, carrying the scent of wildness. He slid from the bed, came across to stand in front of her in her chair. She sighed. When she saw that he was about to speak, she reached out to lay her finger across his lips. There had been enough talking. He undid the belt of her dressing-gown, put his hands on her waist. Kneeling between her legs, he leaned forward to kiss her. She closed her eyes, put her arms round him and for a while was happy.

'You must be uncomfortable, bent like that,' she mumbled after a while. 'Let me up and we'll do something better.'

He did as she'd asked. Then, when they were standing face to face, he took the lapels of her gown and eased it from her shoulders till it fell in a froth round her ankles. When he took the hem of her pyjama jacket in his hands she lifted her arms so it slipped over her head. He threw it to one side.

Her heart was pounding harder than ever. There seemed to be a giant rightness to all this, it was as if she had suddenly realised that this, this was what she wanted and needed. Ben was the man for her.

Gently he ran his fingers down the side of her face, over her shoulders and across the swell of her breasts. Unaccountably, her breasts felt heavier. She could feel the excitement pulsing though them. He threw his arms round her then kissed her, with a demand, an urgency that she hadn't experienced before. Her mouth opened under his, she wanted to have him all.

He was still wearing his shirt. She could feel the stiffness of her nipples against the cotton of it. 'I want to feel your skin,' she moaned, and pulled at the white garment.

'You shall,' he muttered hoarsely back. 'You shall feel all of me if you wish.' Then his hands were on her hips and the bottom of her pyjamas joined the little heap of clothes round her ankles. He picked her up bodily—she marvelled at his strength. He swung round, gently lowered her onto the bed.

Through half-closed lips she watched him. There was the rustling as he dragged off his clothes. Then the bed dipped and he was by her side, an arm under her head as he gathered her to him.

She took joy in the togetherness of their bodies. All her senses seemed heightened. There was the warmth, the scent of his body. There was the faint roughness of his chin on her cheek—he hadn't shaved since morning and she loved it. Their bodies were naked to the breeze from the open window, and as it eddied round them the coolness only served to excite the warmth of their passion.

Obviously he agreed with her. There was to be no more talking. But his lips—and hers—were everywhere. She hadn't known that there were so many places she could kiss and be kissed.

She felt his mounting desire for her, knew that it only matched her own. Suddenly he was with her, on top of her, brought there as much by her own demands as his own desire. She welcomed him into her, her heart telling her that this, this was the thing they both had to do. They had been too long without recognising what they both felt. Eventually, together they reached a tumultuous climax. She heard herself sigh with ecstasy just as she heard his groan of delight.

The breeze was cool on their damp bodies as they lay side by side now, still holding hands, still touching.

'Jo, sweetheart,' he said, 'that was so—'

'Please, no talking.' She sighed drowsily. 'Nothing you could say could make me happier than I am right now.'

For perhaps ten more minutes they lay there, supremely content to be together. Then he reached down and pulled the sheet over them. And they slept. Jo slept, more contented than she had done in months.

Ben woke her with a kiss and she smiled up at him sleepily. 'Jo, I must go,' he said. 'It's early morning. There's your reputation to think of. I don't want you being talked about.'

'It's my reputation,' she mumbled. 'But, still, perhaps you should come out of your own bedroom in the morning.'

'I'm just thinking of you. Jo, about last night…'

'Last night was wonderful,' she told him. 'I'll never forget it and I hope we do it again soon. But we're not going to talk about it. I'm tired of talking. Now, off you go and I'll see you at breakfast.'

'But, Jo, we—'

'No! No more talking. Just be happy with what we have. I am.' When he still seemed to want to stay and talk, she added, 'You're right. I wouldn't want anyone to see you coming out of my room.'

That decided him. He kissed her once again and then left.

After he'd gone she couldn't sleep. For ten minutes she tried to doze, but then she got up, bathed and dressed. She made herself a cup of coffee and then thought of phoning Ben's room. Perhaps not. It could only complicate things.

There was still an hour before breakfast so she decided to go for a walk. The morning was wonderful, the view across the still lake breathtaking. She sat on an upturned boat—the one she had been in the night before—and tried to think how her life had changed.

With the smallest of shocks she realised what she had done the night before. It was something *she* had initiated.

She had made love to—with—Ben. Of course, she had made love to Harry, but she had been expecting to marry him, and she had no thoughts of marrying Ben. The most wicked of thoughts slipped into her mind. Comparisons might be evil, but Ben was a more considerate lover than Harry, and had made her far happier. She decided that wasn't a good way to think.

So, she had no thoughts of marrying Ben—in fact, she had no thoughts about the future at all. She didn't want to plan, to look ahead. She had done that once already, and it just wasn't worth the risk. Ben was good for her, good to her. But she had no long-term plans involving him. She would live one day at a time.

She sat there a while longer, enjoying the crispness of the morning air, the mist eddying round the distant peaks. Only when she knew it was time for breakfast, and set off back to the hotel, did another thought strike her. She knew what she wanted out of this relationship. Did she know what Ben wanted?

She saw him at breakfast, but he had been outmanoeuvred by the indefatigable Eleanor and she wasn't able to sit next to him. However, they sat next to each other during the morning's first lecture, and he squeezed her hand. But he paid full attention to what was being said, and she admired him for that.

After the first lecture they separated for different workshops and seminars. It was another hard session—but she enjoyed it.

The morning finished with a short plenary session and then there was a massive exchanging of addresses. Each delegate got a large goodie bag. Jo saw that, as well as the usual pamphlets, technical details and promotional material, there were the usual gifts—a writing set and a very smart leather briefcase.

'D'you want to stay here for lunch or shall we stop somewhere on our own?' Ben managed to ask her.

'Somewhere on our own. See you at the car in ten minutes?' In fact she managed to get to the car in plenty of time, Ben was a quarter of an hour late. 'Nice to be popular.' She grinned at him.

They set off through back roads and eventually came to a pub advertising lunches. It was still warm so they sat outside and ate sandwiches and drank shandy. She felt perfectly content.

'You stopped me talking earlier,' he said, 'but something must be said. Last night I—'

'Last night was wonderful,' she interrupted. 'It's not going to stop us being friends, just because we've been lovers. We're still going to be able to work together. I'm not going to make demands on you. You're good to me, Ben, and that's what I want and need. But I hope that you'll want to make love to me again.'

'I certainly do.' He frowned. 'I know how you feel, but remember I've got feelings too. I've got feelings, for you. But—'

She leaned over the table and kissed him on the lips. 'No buts. We'll make the most of what we have. Together, no strain, no promises. Just don't ever say that you love me.'

There was a silence, then he said, 'If that's what you want.'

It was Monday morning. Andrew, Ben and Jo were having an informal conference in the hospital canteen.

'We've known for years just how effective cryo-surgery can be in removing malignant tissue,' Ben said. 'But the problem has been measuring just how far the effect of the freezing is spreading. What Reardon's have done is develop more effective monitoring. They've designed this very precise imaging system so the surgeon can know exactly which cells he's destroying, which cells he's leaving alive. Cryo-surgery will be less invasive, more exact, and will mean that we spend less time cutting and searching.'

'I think I'm convinced,' Andrew said. 'Give me a couple more days to look through the details you've brought, then I'll be in touch with the hospital secretary and ask for funding. We'll all become cryo-surgeons. Ben, if that comes off, according to the details here, it looks like someone will have to go to Philadelphia for a further fortnight's study. D'you fancy it?'

'I fancy it no end,' said Ben.

'If it's decided, let's celebrate,' Jo said, 'I'll fetch us all another cup of tea.'

As she was waiting in the queue, tray in hand, she saw a man enter the canteen. He was a stranger to her, and looked as if he hadn't been there before. He looked round carefully, then saw the table where Ben and Andrew were deep in discussion. He smiled broadly, and walked towards them.

'Four cups of tea, please,' said Jo.

By the time she got back to the table, Ben and the new man were hugging each other.

She put her tray of tea on the table. 'I got an extra cup,' she said, adding to the stranger, 'Would you like some tea?'

Ben smiled at her. 'This is our scrub nurse, Jo Wilde,' he said. 'You can see how good she is—she knows what we want before we know it ourselves. Jo, this is Rob Simpson, a very good friend of mine. He's going to be a counsellor attached to the hospital. We spent a lot of time together in Birmingham.'

The man took her hand and shook it—a firm but not hard grip. 'Jo Wilde, I'm very pleased to meet you,' he said. 'How did you know I was desperate for tea?'

She laughed as they all sat down. This was the first of Ben's friends that she had ever met, and she knew she was going to like him. He was short and broad, balding a little. But his eyes were alert and his smile invited confidence at once.

'I'm very pleased we've got a counsellor at last,' Andrew said. 'I've said the hospital needed one for some time now.'

'I'm afraid that's an unusual point of view for a

surgeon,' Rob said. 'Too many of them think that the body and the brain are only physical.'

'Not me. I know vast amounts about the brain, but about the mind I know nothing.'

'Where are you living?' Ben asked Rob. 'Got a house or a flat yet?'

Rob shrugged. 'I've just arrived. I'll stay in a hospital room till I get my work sorted out, then I'll look round for somewhere.'

'Perfect! You can stay tonight on my narrow boat. We'll go over old times.'

'That narrow boat! It should have sunk before now. Jo, have you seen his waterborne home?'

'I've been very happy, the couple of times I've been on it,' she said demurely.

Pints of beer in hand, Ben and Rob sat outside the Waterside Inn, happily aware that they had only a few yards to walk to their beds in the narrow boat. They'd had an excellent meal with a bottle of Burgundy, now they could sit and reminisce for a while. They hadn't seen each other for six months as Rob had been in America, studying a new kind of therapy.

'You'll like Kirkhelen better than Birmingham,' Ben said. 'You'll be made very welcome here. Life here has been good to me. I'm learning a lot, working with Andrew. It's a good hospital, we've got a good team together. And now one of my oldest friends has joined me.'

'I'm very much looking forward to being here,' Rob admitted. 'I'm being given very much a free hand to organise my work.'

'There'll be plenty.' Ben sipped his beer. 'Tell me, what did you think of Jo, our scrub nurse?'

The little group had sat and talked for quite a while at lunchtime.

Rob said, 'I think she's very attractive, she has a good sense of humour, she won't be overpowered by senior members of staff. I liked her no end. I take it there's some special reason for that question?'

'Yes. I think I'm falling in love with her.'

Rob smiled with obvious pleasure. 'Great, it's about time. I really do think she's a super girl, and I wondered if there was something between you.'

'I think I'm very lucky. I'll tell you a bit about her story before you hear it from someone else in the hospital. She was going to be married but was jilted a week before the wedding. She was in a pretty bad state. I would have asked you to help her, but you weren't here so I've been trying to help her myself.'

'You've been doing what?' Rob's words were sharp. Ben saw his friend suddenly jerk upright, his body alert.

'I've been counselling her a bit myself. Well, just talking to her really.'

'I see. Have you any training—any knowledge— any experience of counselling?'

The question was edgy, and Ben felt ill at ease. 'Not really. Well, none at all, in fact.'

'What would you say if I walked into your operating theatre, said I wanted to help and could I have a scalpel, please?'

'The two things aren't the same at all,' Ben protested. 'Like I said, I only talked to her and mostly listened to her, as a friend.' He saw Rob carefully settle back in his seat, deliberately relax, and it made him nervous. What had he done wrong?

'You'd be surprised the harm that can be done by "only talking",' Rob said. 'Let's get things straight. I take it this was to be a big wedding—church, reception and so on—and the husband to be broke it off a week before the ceremony?'

'Yes. And on the actual wedding day she ran in front of a car and broke her leg. She had to have quite a long stay in hospital.'

'Broke her leg! This gets worse. So she was upset to start with, and then the trauma of a major accident and a long stay in hospital. No formal counselling, but a good friend does what he can.'

'She wasn't really a friend to start with, just an acquaintance. We'd only just met.'

'So a friendly, good-looking man wants to talk to her, help her think about her problems, talk them through. Just how intimate has your relationship got, Ben?'

'That's none of your business!' Ben snapped.

'I think it is, Ben. I think it's very much my business. And you've answered my question. Look, you're about to get angry. Well, don't. There are things here we have to get sorted out. For Jo's sake as well as yours.'

Ben drank more beer. 'All right, I'm calm now.'

'I'm not diagnosing, I'm talking about possibilities. Ever heard of transference? It can happen often between counsellor and patient. If a person is in love, and the object of that love is wrenched away—say by death or, in this case, by desertion—then there's a danger that that love will focus on the next most convenient person. Very often the counsellor. And remember, a person being counselled is, above all, vulnerable.'

'I didn't take advantage of Jo's weakness,' Ben snarled. 'I only tried to help her, as a friend. Can't you understand that?'

'Why are you angry? Why are you shouting at me?' Rob asked calmly. 'It couldn't be that you feel slightly guilty, could it?'

Ben clutched his glass in both hands, said nothing. After a while he bowed his head. 'I'd forgotten how hard you can be,' he said. 'Have you anything more to say?'

Rob paused and took a breath, then said, 'Just one last small thing, and it's harder than anything I've said so far. The relationship between a counsellor and a patient should be the same as that between a doctor and a patient.'

To this, Ben could say nothing. After a while, Rob reached across the table and shook his friend's shoulder. He said, 'Of course, there's a very good chance that I'm completely wrong. All I suggest you do is think through what I've said. I shan't ever mention it again unless you do.'

'I think I've had enough beer,' said Ben. 'Would you like to go and see if you can get us a pot of coffee?'

When Rob had gone he lifted his head and stared at the stars overhead. They were far away. That was what he needed now—some distance from his own feelings.

He was a sensible, cautious surgeon, capable of the detachment necessary to take the most difficult decisions. Quite often he had to calculate terrible odds. Should he excise a tumour so a patient could live a happy fulfilled life—if they survived the surgery? Now he needed the same detachment to think about his own life—and it wasn't easy.

He ran through in his mind what he had done, what his motives had been, when—if at all—they had changed. Certainly all he had wanted at first had been to help Jo. Or had he? He remembered how attractive he had always found her. When had he started to fall in love with her? He wasn't sure himself.

Rob had returned and was pouring two mugs of coffee. Ben took one and said, 'it hurt, but I appreciate what you did, Rob. I'd like your help. But there are two people's emotions to be considered here. I'm getting…very fond of Jo. But I'm not sure what she feels about me.'

'I never doubted that you were sincere,' Rob said. 'I think you're a very good, caring doctor. And what's between you and Jo might be fine, I just don't know. But I would hate you to be caught in a situation in which one or the other of you realised in a few months that your relationship was based on a mistake.'

'So what do I do?' Ben asked. 'I just can't give her up.'

'I'd like to talk to her,' said Rob. 'If she wants to talk to me, that is. I'll explain what might have happened. I'll suggest that you can still be friends, can work together, but that for a while you hold back on the strength of the relationship…until she's stronger.'

'Sounds like it might be for the best,' said Ben gloomily.

CHAPTER SIX

'I DON'T like being talked about behind my back,' said Jo, 'especially by someone who I thought was my friend.'

She was sitting in Rob's new office, surrounded by packing cases and stacks of unsorted books, and she wasn't enjoying herself.

'If you want, you can walk out of here now and you'll never hear another word about it from me. But, believe me, Jo, I only want to help you and my friend Ben.'

Jo felt ill at ease. It was only the day after she had met Rob for the first time. She had talked with Ben briefly this morning and he had seemed uncomfortable, upset. Her sister was going out that evening and she had intended to invite Ben round for a meal. Instead, he had suggested she come and talk to Rob when the day was over. So here she was—and she would much rather have had Ben with her.

'Exactly what are you suggesting?' she demanded. 'That I don't know what I'm doing? That I can't recognise my own feelings?'

'Feelings can deceive us. I'm sure you know that.'

'Yes, I know it. I know it very well. Anyway, why d'you think my feelings are involved? Perhaps all I want is simple sex.'

'Sex is never simple,' he said. 'And I'm pretty sure

that you eventually would end up in some sort of a relationship. I know you're that sort of girl.'

She looked at Rob with some dislike. 'You know, I was beginning to enjoy life again. Largely because of Ben. Now you've come along and spoiled things for us. So tell me, what d'you want me to do?'

'If you'll have me, I'd like to be your counsellor. All we'll do is talk about things. But I'm never going to tell you what to do. In time you might find that you're certain that you know what you're doing, that you're happy with Ben. Incidentally, he's been my friend for a long time. I think he's a wonderful man and any woman who gets him will be very lucky.'

'It's easy to see whose side you're on,' she said crossly, and he laughed.

'All I want you to do is to think about your own feelings,' he said. 'I want you to tell me about Harry.'

'I've already forgotten him!'

'And three months ago you were going to spend the rest of your life with him. What will you think about Ben in three months?'

'You're a smart fellow, aren't you?' she said after a pause. 'All right, I'll go along with what you say. But I've got to work with Ben. If I can't work, my life—'

'I want you to work with Ben and I want you to continue being his friend. But perhaps you might decide not to be too…committed for a while.'

'You mean don't sleep with him,' she said brutally.

Rob grinned. 'I'm going to enjoy working with you. You don't mess around. Shall we arrange another appointment'

Jo drove home, and after her sister had gone out she

picked up the phone and started to dial Ben's number. Then she stopped. She didn't know what to say. Twice more she tried before she managed to dial the full number.

The phone was snatched up at once. 'Jo, it's so good to hear from you. How did it go?' His voice was anxious.

'He gave me quite a lot to think about,' she said. 'I like him, he's shrewd. About us—'

Ben interrupted. 'Let me say something first. I think an awful lot of you, Jo. I think we could have something worth fighting for.'

'I agree! Well, I think I agree. Ben, I'm confused again. But we'll get things sorted out.'

'We're still friends, though? We'll still see each other?'

'We'd better be. Who else am I going to turn to to sort out my problems if I can't get help from my friends?'

He laughed. 'I think you're wonderful,' he said.

The next two weeks were…odd. The first thing Jo did was tell Kate about Ben and Rob. Surprisingly, Kate strongly supported Rob. 'I like Ben a lot, an awful lot,' she told Jo. 'He's going to be good for you. But what this Rob fellow says makes sense. Ben will wait, because you're worth waiting for. And if you're more certain, then you'll be happier.'

'I haven't seen you and Steve do much waiting.' Jo said sourly, then giggled when Kate blushed.

In fact, she managed to see quite a lot of Ben. They still worked well together. They had coffee and lunch together. But the only time she went back to the narrow boat for a meal, Rob came as well. 'I don't know whether I'm a chaperon or the referee,' he announced, and they all laughed. It was a good trip.

Her meetings with Rob were surprisingly fruitful. He made her think about Harry in far more detail than Ben ever had, and she was amazed at what emotions he managed to uncover. She had felt them, but had never realised it. He got her to face up to her anger, to her feelings that she had been belittled by what had happened, to her feelings of blame.

'This is terrible,' she said after a while. 'I thought all my thoughts would be of Ben, seeing as we'd just...started something. But I seem to be dealing with, well, all sorts of stuff from my past.'

'So what do you feel for Ben now? I saw you this morning, having a friendly chat in the canteen.'

She thought. 'Well he's there. He's solid. I know that he's waiting for me so I've got something to look forward to. I think I almost...well, I'm very fond of him.'

'I wondered what you were going to say then,' Rob murmured, but he didn't press her.

Jo also took great pleasure in the fact that her sister's relationship was going really well. She knew that Kate wanted a big wedding. She also knew that Kate wouldn't even mention it while there was any chance of her remembering her own cancelled ceremony.

'You promised I could be your matron of honour,' she said. 'Well, I don't mind settling for being chief bridesmaid.'

'Plenty of time,' Kate said calmly. 'Anyway, why should I want to move out of here? I'm very comfortable.'

* * *

There was a letter waiting for Jo when she went in for coffee next morning. She often received mail through the hospital, but mostly it tended to be professional, firms wanting her to buy equipment or sign on for pension schemes. But this seemed different. When Ben passed it to her he showed her that he had one exactly like it, addressed in a bold, clear handwriting. They opened the letters together. They were invitations from a sixth-form student, asking them to give a talk to her college's supper club.

'What d'you think Jo?' Ben asked as he too finished reading.

She pondered. 'For a start, it's a very well-written letter. I've heard of St Luke College. It's about ten miles away and it's getting a good name. I've got nothing on that evening. I think I'd like to do it. What about you?'

He grinned. 'I'll come. This will be the second talk we've done together. We'll be getting a name, all sorts of people will be asking us to speak.'

She shrugged. 'I think it's possibly good for me. And I had a good schooling, I'd like to give a bit back. D'you think Rob will mind us going together?'

'We're going as friends,' he said softly. 'Jo, I still love your company.'

'OK. I'll phone to say we're coming. But first I think I'll phone the headmistress.'

She did phone and recognised the voice on the other end of the line at once. The lady had attended their previous talk a few weeks ago. 'Miss Wilde? How good of you to call. I take it you want to talk about Ruth Rowlands's letter, but first of all I want to apologise to you.'

'There's no need to apologise. Ruth's was a very well-written letter.'

'No, it's not that. At the lunch club I was the person who asked you about working with handsome young men. I meant it as a joke, a happy way to finish the meeting—but it went wrong, didn't it?'

'It was a fair question,' Jo said with some difficulty, 'and I tried to answer tactfully.'

'In the circumstances it was brilliant. But before you answered you bent your head and squeezed the table edge. In my job you have to watch body language, understand it. It was a very bad question for you, wasn't it? It was painful and I'm sorry.'

'You're very astute, Miss Jackson. Yes, you weren't to know, but it was a bad question. I was jilted a few weeks before the talk. Just before my wedding.'

'Ah. I see.' The voice was full of pain. 'I'm so sorry. And I can feel for you—the same thing happened to me.'

Jo would have liked to have known more, but decided this wasn't the time. 'Miss Jackson, Dr Franklin and I would both like to come to the supper club next Friday.'

'I'm so glad!' Miss Jackson's delight was obvious. 'Ruth will also be delighted. She's a wonderful girl and she runs that supper club so efficiently. Did she mention that she wanted to be a doctor herself?'

'No,' said Jo, 'but we need doctors who can organise.'

'I'm sure. Did she say anything else…about herself?'

Jo could tell there was something in the voice. 'Not

at all,' she said. 'What else is there she should have said?'

'Oh, nothing. She's hard-working, bright, a good mixer, a keen sportswoman. You'll like her.'

'Miss Jackson, you're holding something back.'

She heard the headmistress laugh. 'If I am, it's nothing to Ruth's detriment. Make up your own mind. By the way, you won't see me or any of the staff at the club. Ruth and her committee do all the organising themselves. And that's a good thing. But I hope we meet again some time, Miss Wilde.'

'I hope so, too,' said Jo. She replaced the receiver and looked at Ben.

'We're going,' she said. 'I was impressed by the headmistress—but she's keeping something back.'

'We'll find out,' said Ben.

Ben drove Jo to the college. Summer was ending now. Although it was still sunny there was an edge to the air, a rawness in the slight breeze. They had been sent directions, and eventually came to a low, custom-built building on the outskirts of a small town. They drove into the inner courtyard and parked as instructed. It was ten to seven.

In front of them was a set of double doors. Suddenly they bumped open. Towards them came a girl, aged about eighteen. She had long, dark hair and an instantly appealing smile, and her body showed the ripening curves of late adolescence. She was dressed in a sleeveless white blouse, showing firmly muscled arms. She wore a long flowing skirt in blue cotton. And she rolled down the ramp in a wheelchair.

'Hello, you must be Miss Wilde and Dr Franklin. I'm Ruth Rowlands.'

They shook hands, and Jo couldn't think of anything to say except to mumble the usual things. But Ben said, 'Miss Jackson said you were an athlete. Don't tell me, you throw the javelin?'

Ruth's eyes widened with pleasure. 'How clever of you! Yes, I throw the javelin. In time I hope to represent England in the Paralympics. And I've done a couple of half-marathons in this thing.'

'Must have made your hands ache,' said Ben. 'I understand you want to be a doctor?'

'Yes. It might be a mad ambition, but that's what I want.'

'A mad ambition because you're in a wheelchair?' Ben asked. 'It's not impossible but it will make things harder.'

At first Jo was shocked at the sheer brutality of the question. Then she realised this was what Ruth needed. Not to be pitied, not to be ignored, but to be understood. It was typical of Ben that he realised that.

'I know it'll make things difficult,' Ruth said, 'but I've found a couple of medical schools which will take me if I get the grades.'

'You're in the wheelchair for good?' Ben was still casual.

'At the moment, that's the accepted fact. I was knocked down by a drunk driver five years ago. The usual story—nerves in my spine were damaged and can't be repaired. Perhaps…perhaps in the future there might be a wonderful new treatment. You get stories from America, experiments and ideas…but the thing to do is ignore the future and get on with the present.

Now, come inside and meet the other man who's going to be speaking this evening. He's my GP, Dr Luke Sinclair, and since I see a lot of him I guess I've blackmailed him into coming here.'

Ruth wheeled round and led them inside to a small staffroom where there was a pot of tea waiting. They were given tea and introduced to Dr Sinclair—a pleasant blond young man about Jo's age.

'Now,' Ruth said, 'we've got five minutes before the meeting starts. Dr Franklin, can I take advantage and ask you a couple of questions? I've been reading up about the cerebral cortex and I...'

It was a complex question so Jo let Ben get on with explaining. Luke drew Jo to one side and whispered, 'That girl comes to me technically for treatment and spends all her time asking me questions I can't answer. I have to put her on the end of my list so I can overrun into my dinner hour.' But he smiled as he spoke, and Jo knew he was happy with the situation.

'You like being a GP?' she asked.

'It's what I always planned. I never wanted to work in a hospital, there's too much throughput. You never get to know people. Here, if I go to the pub, people know who I am. Mind you, they do tend to come up during my second pint and tell me about their ailments.'

Jo laughed. She liked Dr Luke Sinclair.

It was time to start the meeting. Jo realised she wasn't feeling nervous—this was nothing like giving the talk in Riston. She had grown stronger, more self-confident. In fact, she was quite looking forward to the next two hours.

She had been aware of a growing hum from next

door, of the clatter of feet. Their audience was waiting. Ruth opened a door and led the three into a lecture theatre.

It was a bit fearsome to see forty or fifty people banked up in front of her, many of them holding notebooks. There were both sexes, evenly distributed. And all of them dressed so well! Things had changed since Jo was a schoolgirl.

There was instant silence when Ruth rolled to the front. This was an attentive audience. She gave a brief introduction and then Luke Sinclair spoke first. He was good. He talked about the continuity of a GP's life, the chance of meeting people, the fact that he worked as a member of a team. Not just doctors, but nurses, health visitors, counsellors, midwives, physiotherapists. What he hated most was when his instructions—not suggestions—were ignored. Antibiotics were getting less effective because people just wouldn't finish the prescribed course. But he would recommend a GP's life to anyone.

Ben came next.

'Sometimes, when I'm about to start an operation, I stand there with a patient below me on the table. But all I can see is a patch of bare skin, surrounded by cloths. There are lights overhead, an entire team of helpers waiting to do whatever I want them to. There's a scalpel in my hand. And it's almost impossible to make the first cut through skin, fat and muscle. But I have to do it. And after that things are fine.'

Jo could tell that the audience was fascinated. Ben had got them.

He went on to tell them that much of a surgeon's work was done before the patient ever got to Theatre.

The parts played by ancillary staff—X-ray technicians, nurses, the laboratory itself—all contributed to the final decisions made by the surgeons. Finally, he talked about the loneliness of the job. 'I said I was surrounded by a team of helpers. But there are some decisions that only I can make. Possibly life-or-death decisions. And they are hard.'

If anything, Ben was clapped even harder than Luke. Jo realised that coming last wasn't perhaps such a good idea. People would make comparisons. Still, she would do what she could.

She started with the same three sentences she had used when talking to the lunch club, and she thought they went down well. After that she concentrated on talking about the responsibilities and the teamwork. She mentioned the pleasure they all got when someone benefited from an operation and, since no one had talked about it yet, talked about the feeling of personal grief when someone actually died. She could see this interested the audience. When she had finished Jo was applauded generously, too. She felt proud of herself.

As Ruth had said in her letter, the questions afterwards were most important. There were a few technical questions, quite a lot of moral ones.

One was specifically for Jo—would she ever now consider training to be a doctor?

'No. I think doctors' and nurses' jobs are complementary. You can't have one without the other—and I've picked the one that I'm comfortable with.'

Dr Luke then said, 'I'd like to add that over the past few years more and more of what were considered doctors' jobs have been taken over by nurses—often

very successfully. I can see the two professions growing closer, perhaps becoming more equal.'

The questions were still coming when Ruth moved
to the front of the room and said, 'We must have some
mercy on our guests. Sorry, but there's time for only
two more questions. The questions came and Ruth
closed the meeting, asking a rather quiet girl out of
the front row to propose a vote of thanks. The girl was
nervous, and Jo felt for her. She had noticed how carefully the girl had taken notes. She was obviously interested but hadn't asked a question herself. But her
little speech was read out carefully, and then, after
more clapping, the guests were invited to move first
to another room to have supper.

It was good. The students had done well, utilising
the food and technology department's facilities. Jo
took a roll and a glass of orange juice and looked for
the girl who had proposed the vote of thanks.

'I'm Julie Gray,' the girl said when asked. 'I was
thinking of training to be a nurse, perhaps a children's
nurse. I could never do what you do. And I couldn't
nurse adults. I'm not confident, not like Ruth there.'

'You get confident when you're prepared,' Jo said.
'I remember the first injection I had to give. I was
nervous but it went well because I'd practised, I was
prepared. Remember what Dr Franklin said about having to make the first cut with a scalpel. If a doctor as
experienced as he is can feel nervous, then you're entitled to as well. Just don't sell yourself short.' She
grinned and went on, 'And nursing children is much
harder than nursing adults!'

'Thanks,' said Julie. 'I'll think about that.' She did
look more thoughtful.

Jo went back for another roll. She noticed that there was still a tight knot of students round Ben, but Luke suddenly appeared by her. 'I enjoyed your talk,' he said. 'Do you do them often?'

'No, I don't speak often, this is only the second time. But you seem to be quite practised. Are you?'

He nodded. 'I do quite a bit and I do some writing, too. I think there's a lot a GP can get across to an audience that he can't say to an individual. And since I'm not married or engaged or anything, I have some spare time. Are you married or anything, Jo?'

That was cleverly done, she thought with an inward smile, but merely said, 'I was engaged until recently, but it fell through. I think I'm happy being single for now. Tell me about the writing you do.'

From his pocket he took a slim book and handed it to her. It was called *A Doctor's Week*, and was illustrated by fairly complex drawings. But the writing seemed... She couldn't work it out.

'These books are designed for adults who are learning to read,' he explained. 'They're also used to teach English as a second language. I use a limited vocabulary and the simpler grammatical constructions. At the end...' he showed her '...we introduce twenty-five new words. There's a big need for books like this. Adults don't want to read children's books, they're often not stupid. And I can get my ideas about health issues across.'

Jo was impressed. 'Have you written many?'

'Five so far, all on medical subjects. But my publisher wants more—he says they're selling well.'

'I want to thank you again for coming, Miss Wilde.' Ruth had come up to speak to them. 'That was one of

the most exciting meetings we've had. I hope you enjoyed it as much as we did.'

'I enjoyed myself no end,' Jo said sincerely. 'I hope
you got something out of it.' She looked up to see
Ben. 'Are we going now?'

'Dr Sinclair here is running Ruth back. I think it
might be an idea if we left so that they can clear up
after us. Ruth, I'll be in touch.'

Jo shook hands with Ruth and Luke and walked
with Ben out of the building. Behind them they could
hear Ruth efficiently directing the clearing away of
what remained of the food.

'Enjoy yourself?' he asked as they made towards
his car.

'Surprisingly, very much so. Haven't schools
changed recently?'

'Not a blazer or gym slip in sight,' he said gloomily.
'I don't know where it will all end. Look at that sky!'

She did so. A hard-edged black cloud was creeping
across the heavens, hiding the stars. 'It's going to
rain—and hard,' she said.

Ben avoided the main roads on the way back, but
went cross country, taking narrow bending roads
through the fields. Occasionally a few heavy drops of
rain spattered on the windscreen. 'It's still quite early,'
Jo said. 'You could come round to my place and have
another cup of tea. Kate's in, we'd be quite safe.'

'No love-making?' he asked hopefully.

'Certainly not! Perhaps a chaste kiss on the cheek
when you leave.'

'Better than nothing, I suppose. Are you finding this
as hard to keep up as I am?'

'Probably harder. But I can see Rob's reasoning.

He's taught me one thing. I was too…focussed on you. Perhaps I was interested in you just for what I could get out of you—emotionally, I mean. Rob said that I'll be ready when I can give emotionally as well as take. It's a valuable lesson.'

By her side Ben sighed and shook his head. 'And I thought anyone could be a counsellor. I must have been mad to try.'

'Ben, I was grateful, and you helped me,' she said. 'Don't ever forget that.'

They were silent for a moment or two and she found her thoughts drifting to Luke Sinclair, what he had said to her, how she had responded. She now realised he had quite taken to her. She hadn't meant to encourage him and hoped he hadn't taken anything she had said the wrong way.

She saw a set of lights coming towards them. Ben slowed the car. He, too, couldn't quite make out what the vehicle was. The road here was lonely, narrow, with sharp bends. It would be too easy to be surprised. Then they saw that it was a giant tractor moving slowly towards them, pulling a machine she couldn't quite recognise.

'They've been gathering potatoes,' Ben said. 'When they're ready and it's fine, you have to work all day. It's hard work in the wet.' A moment later they passed the machine and accelerated away.

Half a mile further on they came to the entrance to the potato field, it was on a bend. There was thick, clayey mud all over the road. Ben slowed again but Jo still felt the tyres slip as they took the curve. 'Dangerous,' Ben said.

Then it rained. It rained as it had threatened to do,

a sudden, massive downpour that battered the car roof so loudly she could hardly hear herself speak. Yet again Ben slowed. Both knew that this was merely a squall. And a moment later, as suddenly as it had started, the rain stopped.

'We're having an exciting night,' she said.

The road stretched on ahead of them, curving, undulating. After a couple of hundred yards the surface was dry—the squall hadn't reached this far. And just as she noticed this, there was the sight of a single headlight racing towards them. They heard the roar of an engine and a motorbike was flashing past them. They had a momentary glimpse of the rider, head down, body nearly flat against the tank, his pillion passenger clutching him round the waist, blonde hair flowing from under the helmet. Then the bike was gone.

Gently, Ben let the car roll to a stop. He switched off the engine, wound down the window. 'What are you doing?' she asked him.

He didn't answer at first, then he said, 'I'm a doctor. I shouldn't go looking for trouble, it comes to me anyway. That motorcyclist is entirely capable of making his own decisions. I think he was going too fast. Perhaps he knows better. But any minute now he's going to hit a sharp bend where there's mud all over the road and rain on top of it. On two wheels you won't be safe going any faster than fifteen miles an hour. And there'll be a car along here only once every hour. But it's his decision and perhaps I've seen too many motorcyclist brought in with—'

'Turn round,' she said. 'It's only ten minutes out of

our lives and you won't be happy otherwise. Besides, I want to go back, too.'

They turned. There was no sign of the bike on the bend. Then Jo pointed to the mud on the road. A great furrow ran across it, leading to a growth of bushes.

Ben reversed, switched on his hazard lights and pointed his headlights at the bushes. He fetched a torch out of the boot. Then he and Jo ran to where the furrow ended. As they got closer they could see that some branches of the bushes were broken, though most had sprung back. By the light of Ben's torch they peered through the bushes. There was a ditch on the other side. In it was the motorcycle. Sprawled above it on the bank were two still figures. The rider had taken the corner too fast.

Ben pulled his mobile from his pocket and thrust it at Jo. 'Phone for an ambulance and then fetch the bag out of my boot.' He pushed through the bushes. Jo stood there and dialled 999. She could just see the two figures. The boy was ominously still, but the girl, who was lying on top of the bank, moved as she watched.

The emergency service receptionist was calm, re-assuring. Jo repeated their location twice and then ran to fetch Ben's bag. Quite a lot of doctors carried bags for emergencies. Just how much equipment Ben would have she didn't know. She grabbed the bag and pushed herself through the bushes to join Ben, squatting by the girl's side.

The accident could only have happened minutes ago. If there had been any serious injuries, then the next five minutes were vital. Even an apparently minor injury could result in death. The first thing she knew was to check ABC—airway, breathing, circulation.

The girl was lying on her back, the long blonde hair they had seen earlier now trailing through the mud. Jo saw mud and scratches on the side of the helmet where it had ploughed into the bank.

Fortunately the girl was lying on her back. Perhaps they wouldn't need to move her. Even more fortunately, her helmet was of the type that had a full hinged front. They were able to unfasten it and then slide it off. Both of them knew that injury to the spine was possible. The smallest movement could make things worse. But they had to check her airway and breathing.

The girl appeared to have no problem with her airway. She was breathing steadily. Jo checked her watch and counted—seventeen breaths in fifteen seconds. Sixty-eight breaths a minute—well within normal limits and she wasn't hyperentilating.

As they leaned over her, the girl's eyes flicked open and she started to moan. 'What happened?'

'Just lie still,' Jo said. 'You had an accident but you're in good hands now. Just try not to move.'

She saw Ben pull off one of the girl's gloves and take her radial pulse. Then he leaned forward, gently eased down the girl's sweater and placed his fingers on her carotid artery. 'Blood pressure seems to be good enough,' he murmured to Jo. 'I'll just look at her fingernails.'

Jo held the torch as he compressed the fingernail beds for five seconds. When he let go, the pinkness returned in two seconds. Capillary refill time was good. So far the girl seemed to have got off lightly. There was a good chance she wasn't haemorrhaging internally.

Suddenly, the girl tried to get up and Jo held her down. 'You mustn't move,' she said. 'There's an ambulance coming. Just lie still.'

She directed the torch as Ben made a quick survey of the rest of the girl's body. There were no obvious signs of bleeding, no bent limbs. Jo looked at the surroundings, tried to assess what had happened. If the motorbike had skidded through the bushes and dropped into the ditch, the girl might have been thrown forward to land on the bank. But the boy was lying on the side of the ditch closer to the motorbike. He had hit harder.

'I don't think there's anything seriously wrong here,' Ben said. 'But keep an eye on ABC and make sure she doesn't move. I'll put a collar on her, and we'll wait for the ambulance. OK if I take the torch?'

'No problem,' said Jo.

Jo could tell the girl was coming to. She was breathing more steadily now and there were little twitches of the muscles. Jo knew she'd be in shock, frightened, confused. There was no way she could offer her the traditional hot, sweet drink—even if she had one, it would be lunacy when there was the possibility of anaesthesia later. But at least she could offer comfort.

'What happened?' the girl asked. 'Where's Tommy? I told him he was going too fast but he...' She started to cry and in the dim light of the headlights Jo could just see the tears rolling down the white cheeks.

'You're going to be all right,' Jo said reassuringly. 'I'm a nurse and that man there is a doctor. What's your name?'

'I'm Karen Smith. What'll me mam say? She

doesn't like Tommy and she doesn't like motorbikes. She'll— And what's this round my neck?'

'That's in case you might have…strained it. Just keep still, Karen. Tell me, do you hurt anywhere in particular? Can you wriggle your fingers and toes?'

The reply was a little tart, which encouraged Jo. 'I hurt a lot all over. But I don't think anything is broken. I've got feelings in everything.' There was a pause and then she said with growing irritation, 'I told him not to go that fast! I want to get up and see him.'

'No, Karen! You lie perfectly still! We don't know if you've injured your spine.'

Karen instantly knew what that meant and there was terror in her voice. 'So I could be paralysed?'

'I very much doubt it,' Jo said gently. 'But you will promise me to lie still while I look at Tommy, won't you?'

'I promise,' Karen said with feeling.

Jo scrambled over to help Ben, knelt at the boy's side. 'His name's Tommy,' she said. Somehow, knowing his name made him more of a person. 'Shall I hold the torch for you?'

'Please. The girl all right?'

'Conscious now, and she knows enough not to try to move. How're you doing here?'

'Just keep the head straight, will you? I don't like doing this, but…' Tommy's helmet wasn't hinged, and to get it off Ben had to lift the head. But they had to be able to check ABC. The minute the helmet was removed he slipped on a collar, fortunately having brought two.

The airway was clear—but the breathing was very

rapid. Something was wrong. 'See if you can get to his chest, will you? I'll just check circulation.'

Jo managed to unzip the heavy jacket, then took a pair of scissors from Ben's open bag and cut open the front of the sweater underneath and the T-shirt under that. Then she pushed back the clothing as far as it would go. They daren't lift Tommy up to pull off the clothes.

When she directed the torch downwards they saw signs of abrasions and bruising across the side of the chest. Ben frowned. 'I would guess that he smashed into the handlebars before being thrown over the top,' he said. 'That's going to be a nasty injury. I wonder if...'

Hastily he examined the chest, palpating, percussing, then taking out his stethoscope.

'Breathing's getting more rapid,' said Jo, 'and his pulse is getting even faster but it's very weak.'

Tommy chose this moment to come to full consciousness. 'How's...how's Karen?' he asked.

'She's a bit shaken but she's going to be OK. Now, you lie still, the doctor's examining you. How d'you feel?'

'My chest hurts, and it's hard to breathe. And I'm feeling tired. I...'

'He's lost consciousness again,' Jo reported. 'What's wrong, Ben?'

She thought she knew, but it wasn't up to her to offer an opinion to a doctor—well, not unless she thought he'd got things wrong.

'Tension pneumothorax,' Ben said. 'Classic case. There's less air entering the hemithorax and it's hyperresonant. Trachea's deviated, raised jugular pulse. You know what we have to do?'

'I know,' said Jo, and reached into Ben's bag to pass him a 10 ml syringe and a cannula.

The surface of Tommy's left lung had torn. There was a flap opening into the pleural cavity, the space round the lung. Each time Tommy breathed in, air escaped into the cavity. This escaped air pressed down on the lung, ultimately causing it to collapse. If not dealt with, the condition was fatal. Fortunately, the cure wasn't too difficult.

Ben took the proffered syringe and carefully pushed it into the chest. A hiss indicated that the air trapped in the pleural cavity had escaped. Ben slid a cannula over the needle into the cavity, then removed both syringe and needle. The lung should now be able to work more or less properly.

Jo lifted her head. 'I can hear a siren.'

'D'you want to go and stand and flag them down? But don't stand on the road—we don't want another accident.'

The blue and white vehicle drew up behind Ben's car, lights flashing like some fairground ride. A moment later a police car arrived. Two paramedics jumped out of the ambulance, trotting to where Jo indicated. Jo now stood well back and watched as Ben gave a quick report and the two young men fetched the stretchers from their vehicle. This was a very specialised form of medicine and these men were experts. As Karen was being loaded into the ambulance she opened her eyes and said to Jo, 'Thanks for what you did. This is the end of motorcycling for me. Tommy either loses that bike or he loses me.'

'Don't think about it now,'

Soon the two injured were fixed in the ambulance and it roared away. A policeman took a quick statement from Jo and Ben and asked if one of them could come to the station when it was convenient. But now they could go. Somewhat deflated, and very slowly, they drove away. The entire episode had only taken twenty minutes.

'Quite a full evening,' Jo said as he drew up outside her house. 'You're still coming in for a drink?'

'I need one,' he said, 'and if you offered me a biscuit I wouldn't refuse it.'

'I could run to a sandwich even.' She thought a moment then said, 'If you don't want to go back to the narrow boat tonight I could find you a couch to sleep on.'

He sighed heavily. 'That's the best offer I've had all week and I'm going to turn it down. You know why, don't you, Jo?'

'You couldn't trust me, you or both of us,' she said.

'Something like that. Tonight I'll sleep at the hospital.'

She wasn't quite sure how she felt—disappointed or relieved. But at least he was coming in for a drink.

Kate was at home, already in her dressing-gown, sitting, reading, in the kitchen. They told her what had happened. 'You folks certainly lead full lives,' she said. 'Just sit there and I'll get you both something.'

'I know what I want,' Jo muttered to herself. Then she saw Ben looking at her. Had he heard her? And if so, did he feel the same way?

CHAPTER SEVEN

JO WAS out visiting friends with Kate on Sunday evening and they didn't come in till late. There was a message for Jo on the answerphone.

'Hi, this is Luke Sinclair. I got your number out of the book. I hope there's only one J. Wilde. I've been thinking. I wonder if you'd like to collaborate with me on one of my little books. If you're interested, perhaps we could have a drink together later in the week. Could you ring me at my surgery?'

Kate had listened with her. 'What's he like?' she asked.

'He's very pleasant, I enjoyed his company. And I'm quite interested in the idea of helping him with a book.'

'Is he interested only in your book-writing abilities?'

'Well, I doubt it,' Jo mumbled.

'Little sister, you know very well that a writing collaboration isn't what he wants. Well, not only what he wants. If you're going to ring him back, then tell Ben first.'

'You like Ben, don't you?' Jo asked.

'Yes,' said Kate, 'I like him a lot. And I don't want you messing things up because you haven't thought them through.'

'I can always trust my sister to tell me when I'm being an idiot.'

Of course, she had always intended to tell Ben. So next day, when they had a moment alone in their little rest room, she said, 'Luke Sinclair phoned me last night, Ben. He wants to meet me for a drink so we can talk about my helping him with one of the little books he writes.'

'That sounds like a good idea,' Ben said interestedly. 'You'd like your name on the back of a book.'

'But I suspect Luke wants more than my help in writing. I think he…might fancy me. He sort of said so when we met first.'

'You're a very fanciable woman,' Ben said. 'I don't blame him.'

'Ben! I know we agreed that we'd hold things back for a while but I… Ben, I want you to be jealous a bit. Try and stop me!'

He shook his head. 'This must be your decision. You must make up your own mind. If you want to go for a drink with him, then go. I thought he was a very personable man. This is the point of us keeping apart. You must do whatever you want to do.'

'But I want you to tell me not to go!'

'No. You must please yourself.'

They were interrupted by Andrew, who wanted a quick word with Ben. Jo was so irritated that she phoned Luke's surgery at once and was put through to him straight away.

'You're interested, great! How about Wednesday night? I'll pick you up straight after evening surgery.'

'All we're having is a talk about a book,' she said. 'I'll drive round to the surgery and pick you up there. It'll save time.'

'As you wish. I'll see if I can get us a table at Madame Leblanc's.'

Jo sighed. He had just mentioned probably the most expensive restaurant in a thirty-miles radius. 'No, Luke. What I want is a friendly chat over a plate of salad or bread and cheese in some local pub. Nothing fancy at all, OK? I'll be wearing my jeans. It's to be that sort of evening.'

'All right, then, if that's what you want.'

As she rang off she wondered if what she was doing was wise.

She couldn't tell Ben what she had done as for the next three days he had been transferred again to a neighbouring hospital. She still felt a little irritated with him. He might have shown *some* indication that he wasn't very happy. But, then, she knew he was doing what he thought was right.

On Wednesday evening Jo picked up Luke and said she would drive. He directed her to a pub on the outskirts of town—it was still quite upmarket. Over a very pleasant seafood platter he showed her the publisher's package, detailing what they required and how the book should be constructed. This interested her and together they started thinking about the new twenty-five words they should introduce in the back of the book. Did people starting to learn to read need to know what a probe was? What about a scalpel? It was fascinating.

She enjoyed herself. Eventually, Luke said that he had enjoyed himself, too and could they meet again next week to talk further—or what about the weekend?

It was time to talk frankly. 'Luke, do you need to

talk to me about the book, or do you just want my company?'

He blinked at her. 'You're very direct,' he said. 'The answer is, yes, I do want to carry on with the book. But mostly I just want to meet you again.'

She sighed. She had got herself into this situation, and it wasn't fair to Luke to string him along any longer. 'I like you, Luke. If circumstances were different, I could like you a lot. But I'm, well, I'm not free. Sorry.'

'Ah. Ben Franklin, is it?'

She nodded.

'He's a very lucky man. I did see him looking at you when you weren't looking at him, and I wondered what it meant but…like I said, he's a lucky man.'

'Thanks, Luke. Look, I'll post you some details next week. I am still interested in the book. Shall I drive you home?'

He shook his head. 'I live quite close. I can walk from here.'

On impulse she leaned over and kissed him. 'Some girl will be very lucky when she gets you,' she said. 'Goodbye, Luke.'

Ben was back next day and Jo wanted to tell him what had happened. As ever, they found themselves in the rest room again, snatching a quick cup of coffee.

'Ben, I went to see Luke Sinclair last night. I enjoyed myself and he did express an interest in me— but I had to tell him that, much though I liked him, I was only interested in collaborating with him on the book.

'I'm glad you had a good time,' Ben said calmly,

'and, yes, I guess that I'm glad that you're not interested in him. But it must be your decision. Don't be
swayed by me.'

This was too much! 'Ben! We're staying apart because of what Rob said! I agreed that we should keep
a bit of distance between us until...until I was sorted
out. But I would have liked just a little indication that
you cared for me. Just a little jealousy would have
cheered me up no end, made me feel wanted. But all
you do is smile and say you're glad I had a good time!
How d'you think I fcel?'

They were in the little rest room, alone at present,
but anyone might come in. In spite of this Ben suddenly grabbed her, pulled her to him and kissed her.
A hard, urgent, kiss.

When he let her go, she saw a rare anger in his face.

Hoarsely he said, 'I had to agree with Rob—that
you needed to stand on your own feet, that I couldn't
act as a sort of emotional shelter for you. Deliberately
I've left you alone. But don't ever ever think that it's
not been hard for me!'

'I'm sorry, Ben,' she whispered.

He turned his back on her and went over to the
coffee-table. She could tell by his hunched shoulders
what he was feeling. But then he took two deep
breaths and she could see the physical effort he made
to calm himself. Then he turned and offered her a mug
of coffee. 'It'll all come right in time,' he said. The
old Ben was back.

Three weeks passed, and Jo felt very much better. She
was clearer in her own mind about what had happened
to her, had even come to remember with some calm-

ness the good times she'd had with Harry. She didn't hate the man any more, he was becoming a memory. She was the old Jo Wilde again, confident, self-assured.

She was practically ready to tell Rob that she thought she had no need of more counselling. Their meetings were no longer the gruelling, soul-tearing sessions they had been to start with. Instead, they seemed to chat gently about her plans for the future. And he asked her advice about where he should live. She was helping him. She knew he was going to be a valued friend.

Then something happened that tore her new found confidence to tatters.

For one day only there were workmen in both the theatres that Jo used. They were installing some of the new cryosurgery equipment Andrew had ordered. 'You've both worked extras hours over the past few weeks,' Andrew had said to her and Ben, 'so have the day off.'

It was a little extra holiday. She had wondered if Ben might suggest they spend the day together, but he had left her a note. Apparently there was something that he had to do urgently.

So she had spend an easy morning, visiting the library, shopping in the centre of town. It was a soft, near autumnal day, and she decided to walk home.

She had walked out of the town centre, and was crossing a small park surrounded by older, Victorian houses. A dark avenue of laurels ran through the centre of the park. She was just coming out of the shade when she heard a woman's voice call out, 'Ben, Ben, it's so good to see you!'

In front of her was an open patch of ground. Across it ran Ben, his face alight with joy. Towards him ran a woman, perhaps a little older than herself and very, very attractive. Ben hugged the woman, picked her up, swung her round and kissed her. There was the kind of tenderness there that only came from a long acquaintance. They wrapped arms round each other's waists, turned and walked away.

For a moment Jo thought she was going to be sick. She couldn't believe the rush of emotions that hit her, the sense of betrayal, the sense of loss and, worst of all, the sense that things were all happening again. First Harry had deceived her. Now Ben was doing the same. Were there no men to be trusted in the world?

She mustn't let them see her. Not that there was much chance, they were walking away and obviously engrossed in each other. She ran back the way she had come and found a bench where she could sit. The tears came and when she searched her handbag for a tissue she found her mobile phone. That was something she could do.

She phoned Rob's direct line. He had now picked a secretary, an older woman who was as compassionate and discreet as himself. 'I've got to talk to Rob,' Jo sobbed. 'I've got to talk to him now. Where is he, Ellie? I've got to talk to him.'

'I'm afraid he's at a meeting,' Ellie said gently. 'No phones allowed in it. Where are you, Jo?'

'I'm at…I'm at Newham Park. I was just walking home and I got…I got a shock.'

'There's a taxi rank just round the corner. Why

don't you get a taxi home? And the minute Rob comes out of the meeting he'll ring you. Can you do that? If you really want, I can fetch him out of the meeting.'

'No…no. Don't do that. I'll do what you say. I'll take a taxi home.'

By the time she got home her shock had worn off slightly and had been replaced by an all-consuming bitterness. She should have known better. Her previous decision had been best—she should concentrate on her work and forget about men.

When the phone rang she considered not picking it up. There was nothing Rob could say to her that would make things better. She was better here, nursing her misery alone. But eventually she answered.

'Ellie said you sounded upset,' Rob's gentle voice said. 'Has anything gone badly wrong, Jo?'

Her voice was so choked that it was a while before she could answer. 'Ben…I saw Ben with another woman. He obviously loves her. I'm never going to trust anyone again, Rob, never. I'm sick of it all. I thought Ben might be different but—'

'This woman,' Rob persisted. 'Was she tall, slim, long blonde hair that's almost silver?'

'You know her! You know all about her! Why didn't you tell me? You're betraying me as well.'

'I'm not betraying you, Jo, you're betraying yourself. That woman is Alice Benson, Ben's cousin, they've known each other since they were babies. Ben and Alice are as close—oh, as you and Kate. And in the same way.'

'He's never mentioned her to me!'

'Alice has an ill child called Michael. Michael is so ill he'll probably die. I imagine Ben didn't mention

Alice and Michael to you because he didn't want to add to your miseries. I'm sure he would have told you in time.'

Jo just couldn't cope with the tumultuous emotions that raged through her. There was relief at having been proved wrong, a relief so great that she could scarcely bear it. There was shame that she had been so ready to condemn without asking. There was pity for Ben and his cousin. And there was horror at herself. She was far, far from being normal.

'I think I'd like to come round to see you. Make me a cup of tea in an hour?'

'I'll be here,' she said. She replaced the phone and burst into tears again.

Rob was coming round and she knew that she ought to talk to him before making any decisions. But some things she had to resolve herself. First she washed her face in cold water. Then she picked up her mobile and phoned Ben's number.

The sound of his cheerful voice sent her heart thumping. Ten minutes before she'd thought that she'd never hear that sound again. 'Jo! It's good to hear from you.'

She hadn't rehearsed what she was going to say, she would just have to say it and hope that everything came out all right. 'Ben, I've done something terrible. I saw you earlier in Newham Park, with…with your cousin. I saw you hold her and kiss her and I thought—'

'Jo! Darling, I never meant for that to happen. Listen, Alice and I, we're just—'

'I know about Alice. I phoned Rob, he told me.'

'So you're happy, you know that Alice and I aren't anything like lovers—though I do love her.'

'I know that. But I'm not very happy with myself.'

'Don't be like that. It was a very natural mistake to make. If I'd seen you with a man as you saw me with Alice, then I'd have felt the same way. She's upstairs now with Michael—he's having a sleep. D'you know about Michael?'

'Rob said he was very ill.'

'He has—had a Wilms' tumour. It was successfully excised from the kidneys, but it was discovered too late. It had metastasised to the lungs and brain. At present it's being treated with chemotherapy, but the tumour in the brain will have to come out when it's been reduced in size. I've asked Andrew if he'll operate, but it's in a very dangerous place. It's deep in the midbrain. I won't be there, of course, but it'll make me feel good if I know you're scrubbing.'

'Ben, I'll do anything to help Michael if I can. But I've just suspected you. An hour ago I hated you. And now you say things like that. You make me feel terrible.'

'That's not what I want to do. Look, I'm taking Alice and Michael on the narrow boat this afternoon. Would you like to come? I'd love it if you would.'

'I couldn't face Alice after what I've thought about her!'

'She's not going to know. And she knows about you, I've told her. She wants to meet you.'

'What have you told her about me?' Jo asked, intrigued.

He laughed. 'That I'm very…taken with you. Shall I pick you up at your house in a couple of hours?'

'No…you'll have enough on. I'll come in the car.'

She felt battered, as tired as if she had swum the Channel or run a marathon. But she felt better. She was glad she had phoned Ben.

So, surprisingly, was Rob. 'Ben's been helping you for a while,' he said when he arrived. 'Now it's going to be your chance to help him. You know what he's like—he gives himself to people.'

'Yes, I know. Is Alice a single mother? Has Michael no father?'

'I think I'll leave Ben to tell you about that,' said Rob.

Ben and his party were already on the boat when Jo arrived. Jo shook hands with the solemn Michael, a big-eyed seven-year-old with a bobble hat covering the bald head caused by chemotherapy. Then she said a shy hello to Michael's mother, Alice. There was no time for long introductions, they would set off at once. Jo was sent to cast off as she had before. Slowly the narrow boat circled through the marina opening and into the canal. Then they were chugging along, the opposite way to the way they'd gone the last time she'd been aboard.

As he had done with her, Ben made a lot of teaching Michael how to steer. The boy was thin, obviously weak, but he responded to Ben's enthusiasm and was a quick learner. Alice went below, said she was making up beds. She refused Jo's offer of help. 'It'll be no great trouble,' she said.

They sailed for half an hour and then Ben cut the engine. 'We'll moor here,' he said. 'If you ladies don't mind being left on your own for a while, Michael and

I will walk through that wood. There's a stream at the other side and I saw a kingfisher there a couple of days ago. Four of us would make too much noise.'

'A kingfisher! Uncle Ben, I'd love to see a king-fisher.'

So Jo and Alice were left together. At first Jo found Alice a little cagey, distant even. Jo didn't mind—she realised that Alice's concern for her cousin was showing through.

'You can't have known Ben very long,' Alice said to Jo. 'He's only been here about four months. Do you see much of him?'

'Well, we work together, we're part of a team, and so we tend to socialise together. We're good friends.'

'I would have thought you were closer than that,' Alice said slyly, and Jo blushed slightly.

'We get on very well,' she said. 'Did Ben tell you anything about my background?'

'He said your fiancé left shortly before your wedding. That was quite a few weeks ago.'

'It seems like a lifetime now,' said Jo. 'I don't think I would have pulled through without Ben. He was just…there.'

'He wrote to me about you but he didn't give any details. Just said that he was happy and had made a good friend.'

'That's nice,' said Jo. 'I like to think of myself as his friend.'

Somehow the other woman's attitude seemed to change. Her body relaxed. 'Yes, he's good like that. Did he tell you anything about me? Or Michael?'

'No, but I'd like to know. If you don't mind telling me, that is.'

'Yes, well. I'm sorry you were let down. Being left like that is heartbreaking. But at least you found out before you got married. My husband walked out after five years. In his letter he said he just couldn't cope with the misery of being Michael's father. Michael was very ill, the tumour and metastases had just been diagnosed. The prognosis…wasn't good.'

'That must have been very hard on you and Michael.' Jo suddenly felt her own problems pale by comparison. 'What did you do?'

'For a long time I thought I'd never cope. But Ben was there and Ben helped me. He's been a carer since he was a little boy, you know. I've been married once, and have no desire to do so again. But if I could find another man like Ben I'd marry him like a shot.'

'You wouldn't marry Ben himself?' Jo just had to ask.

Alice laughed, an obviously genuine laugh. 'I could no more marry Ben than I could my brother—if I had one. I'll tell you a secret, Jo, I was the first female ever to sleep with Ben. But he was two years old and I was eighteen months.'

Jo found herself liking Alice more and more. 'What are you doing in Kirkhelen?' she asked.

'Well, I've rented a house for the moment. Perhaps in time I'll buy one. We're here to get Michael's strength up a bit, then eventually Andrew, your boss, is going to operate on him. Ben has told me that…that this is the best chance for Michael. Chemotherapy can only do so much. It's a risky operation and there's a good chance that it will go wrong. But otherwise he's going to die anyway.' Alice's tone was flat, but Jo could tell the strain she was under.

Jo leaned over to squeeze Alice's shoulder. 'Andrew's a brilliant surgeon,' she said. 'If anyone can pull him through, Andrew will. And I've seen some miraculous results in that theatre.'

She also remembered that there had been operations that hadn't been successful. Operations when the surgeon had pulled off his mask, grey-faced, and had said, 'I'm sorry. There's just no point in going on.'

'What's the house like?' Jo asked. 'Where is it?'

'One of the roads off Newham Park. In fact, it's a nice little place. The landlord is a bit of a DIY fanatic so it's very sound and very well equipped.' Alice laughed again. 'The only trouble is that his taste in wallpaper is, well, eccentric. In fact, it's evil. He likes large purple flowers and broad stripes in strange colours. I didn't want to upset him but I asked if he'd mind if I repainted a couple of rooms. He gave me permission but he wasn't very happy.'

Jo laughed. 'I did a lot of decorating when I—we—bought the new house,' she said. 'I got quite good at it and I've got all the gear still. Shall I come and lend a hand?'

'I'd like that,' Alice said.

'Mum! I saw a kingfisher and it was bright blue like in the pictures in my book and it caught a fish and went down a little hole!'

Ben and Michael were back from their little expedition, and Michael could hardly contain himself.

'Well, I've brought your colouring pens and Uncle Ben has bought you a bird book. Why don't you sit down for a while and colour in the kingfisher? Then we can all look at it.'

'Thanks, Uncle Ben.' Michael obviously thought this was a good idea.

'You two ladies been getting to know each other?' Ben asked, elaborately casually.

'We've been comparing notes. We've got a lot in common, apart from having been helped by you,' Alice said. 'Jo's going to come round and do a bit of decorating with me.'

'That's good,' Ben said, 'that's very good. Let me know when and I'll come and mix the paint for you both.'

They motored on a mile or two further until there was another winding circle and Ben turned the narrow boat round. Then they moored again and had tea. Afterwards Michael was obviously tired, so his mother put him to bed as Ben steered the narrow boat back to the marina. The two were going to spend the night on the boat, as a special treat for Michael.

Ben and Jo sat together in the cockpit. 'You mentioned once that you knew someone who had been taken advantage of,' Jo said, when she was sure they couldn't be overheard. 'Was that Alice?'

'There have been other cases, but Alice's sticks in my mind. She was left quite a bit of money by her parents, being an only child. She's still not too badly off, but her ex-husband got quite a bit of what she had. Now I gather he's trying to marry someone else with money. You know he left her?'

'He said he couldn't cope with Michael.'

'That was only half of it. He couldn't cope with Michael—and he saw a way of getting his hands on the money. So Alice paid him off to get rid of him.' Ben's contempt was obvious.

'I suppose there are worse men than Harry,' Jo said thoughtfully. 'He did leave me the house. Good Lord, I'm even half thinking well of the man.'

'It'll pass,' said Ben.

Confidently she took the tiller as he went along to say goodnight to Michael. When Ben returned, she put her head round the cabin door to whisper goodnight to Alice, who was sitting in the dark with her son, who was almost asleep. When they reached the marina she helped Ben moor the boat. Then he walked her back to her car. It was dusk now, nearly dark. The nights were getting longer.

'This has been a very eventful day,' she said, 'but it's finished with my feeling very happy. Now I don't know if Rob would allow this, but…' She pulled Ben to her and kissed him.

He kissed her back, and she could sense his urgency. But then she felt him pulling away and she laughed.

'You want to kiss me, but you also don't want to risk hurting me,' she said. 'You want to do what's right.'

'I think you're lovely,' Ben said, 'but I want everything between us to be perfect, so I'm willing to wait.'

'You're willing to wait? But are you happy to wait?'

'Oh, no,' he said hoarsely, 'I'm not happy to wait at all.'

The next day Jo asked if she could call to see Rob, not for a proper consultation but just for coffee and a chat. 'I'm feeling much better now,' she said. 'Clearer. 'Yesterday's little episode showed me where I was going wrong. I've learned from it. I'm now a wiser

person. I can put Harry and Ben side by side and compare them without getting instantly upset.'

'So you've learned from everything, have you?'
Rob asked casually. 'You're now just as you were
before you met Harry—no pain, no resentment, no
memory of suffering?'

'Of course not!' She paused. 'You're making a
point, aren't you? What is it?'

'I think you may be wrong. You're not over Harry
yet, your feelings are still confused. It's just that the
greatest healer of all is time. You've not given it too
much. Can you look back at the very best times with
Harry—I know there were some—and not feel upset?'

'No,' she said after a while. 'I still get upset. You're
clever, Rob. But I want to see more of Ben. We seem
to be marking time, getting nowhere, and it's annoying
us both.'

'All right, then, see Ben. But I suggest you don't
rush into things. I hope you don't announce your engagement in a couple of weeks. Getting to know someone you might come to love should be fun. You've
got to find his faults, his hidden virtues, his little odd-
ities. And it's all wonderful. But you mustn't rush to
hide the past by having a great future—it doesn't work
that way. The past is always with you.'

'I'll remember that. And, Rob Simpson, I think at
heart you're just a great big romantic. Shall I still
come to see you? Just occasionally?'

'I hope so. But not for the next fortnight. I'm at-
tending a conference in Switzerland.'

'Come to dinner with us both when you get back.'

*   *   *

That evening Jo went round to help Alice paint. They had arranged it earlier in the day and Jo had promised to bring round the sheets, ladders, brushes and so on that she had saved from when she had decorated her own house.

Alice's house was very pleasant, but the choice of wallpaper was appalling. They started with the living room, pulling the furniture into the centre of the room and covering it with sheets. Michael was sent upstairs to watch TV on a portable set as Alice didn't want him too near the wet paint. Then they started applying the pastel peach paint that Alice had chosen. 'I bought this as a one-coat paint,' Alice said gloomily, 'but I bet it needs two coats.' The purple flowers were showing through.

'It'll be quick with the two of us working,' Jo encouraged. 'We'll get one coat finished tonight.'

There was something therapeutic about painting with another person. They could talk when they felt like it, remain silent if that was their need. 'Ben was telling me that you live with your twin sister,' Alice said after a while. 'That must be great fun. You're very close, aren't you?'

'We look alike, we're close, but we're different,' Jo said. 'For a long time we only had each other—there were no living relations and we were brought up in an orphanage. But Kate is now engaged. She'll get married and Steve will join the family. And I'll like that, too.'

'What's it like, having only one real relation?' Alice asked carefully. 'Do you ever feel lonely?'

'There are good bits and bad bits to only having Kate. Some of the cases we see in hospital, I think our patients would be better off with no family at all. But other families are wonderfully supportive.'

'Has Ben ever talked about his family?'

'Never,' said Jo. 'I thought it was because he knew I had no family, and didn't want me to feel left out.'

Alice carefully painted a corner. 'That might be true,' she said. 'But you know how he's always eager to help people, how he hates bullies, people who abuse power?'

'I thought that was because of you and your husband.'

'True. But only partly true. There's at least one other case. You're very…fond of Ben, aren't you?'

'Yes,' said Jo.

'Then this is something you ought to know. But tell him I've told you, I don't want to go behind his back.'

Jo was intrigued. It struck her that over the past few weeks they had talked a lot about her, but very little about Ben. She wanted to know more about him. 'Go on,' she said.

'Ben's father was Cyril Clement Franklin. He was a brilliant cardiac surgeon in one of the top London hospitals. I knew him—he was my mother's brother. He was also one of the most unpleasant people I have ever met. He was the old style of consultant and surgeon—the kind of man who would throw scalpels onto the floor until the scrub nurse had passed him the right one. He didn't think he was God—he knew it. But as a surgeon there was no one better.

'He alternately bullied and ignored his wife. She was sweet, but she couldn't stand up to him. He had no time for Ben, of course. Ben was a mistake and as soon as possible he was packed off to boarding school.

Ben's mother didn't want that, but her opinion wasn't important.

'Like many women, Ben's mother had problems with the menopause. Her husband was fairly unsympathetic. He spent less and less time at home. And when she was at her lowest, her most vulnerable, her husband announced he was leaving her for someone younger, better educated, better looking. He told her that! So his wife, my sweet Auntie Jane, took an overdose and killed herself. She died through neglect, Jo! But, of course, the verdict was that the balance of her mind was disturbed.'

The sheer horror of this overwhelmed Jo. She put down her paintbrush and turned to look at Alice. 'But…what did Ben say? What did he think?'

'He didn't know till afterwards. And it was over so quickly. His mother didn't want to disturb him at school, he had important exams. But he was old enough, strong enough to help. He still feels guilty that he didn't know, didn't help.'

'How…how did it affect him when he found out?'

'He had a furious row with his father before the funeral, and afterwards told him that in future he'd like to stay at his boarding school in the holidays, there was no point in his coming home. He'd prefer it if they never met again. His father agreed. My mother used to take me to visit Ben at school—we'd bake for him. When he was eighteen Ben was accepted for medical school—he'd done it all without his father's help. He wrote to tell his father but said that there was still really no need for them ever to meet.'

'I think that's the most terrible story I've ever heard,' said Jo. 'Poor Ben! He needs love.'

'He does need love,' Alice said. 'And he deserves it.'

'Did he ever meet his father again?'

Alice smiled sadly. 'There's a typical Ben ending to the story. Ben's father contracted inoperable cancer—in fact, cancer of the brain stem. Ben went and sat with him every night till he died. He couldn't forget—but he could forgive.'

They finished the room by nine o'clock and retired to the kitchen for a swift supper. Michael came down from upstairs. He had heard the sound of talking so he wanted to join in. And at half past nine Ben arrived. Jo wondered at the great swell of happiness she felt when he walked in through the back door.

He had to admire the newly painted room before he was allowed a drink. 'Much better,' he said, 'but I think—'

'Don't say it, we've already decided,' said Alice. 'It needs a second coat.'

When they were all sitting comfortably in the kitchen, Michael said, 'Uncle Ben, can we all go on the boat again? And can Jo come with us as well?'

Ben looked thoughtful. 'Well, I just can't get away before the weekend and I'm flying to America early on Sunday morning. That only leaves Saturday. We can certainly have a little trip then. How are you fixed, Jo?'

Jo frowned. 'I'd love to go. But I told Kate and Steve about that pub you took me to on the canal—you know, the Navigation Inn. They've invited me to go for a meal there with them.'

'D'you think they'd like to go there on the narrow

boat?' Ben asked. 'We could go together as a party. Shall I phone Steve and ask him?'

'That would be great,' Jo said.

Everyone thought it was a great idea. Once again Jo offered to drive everyone to the marina. Not drinking didn't worry her much at all. She liked it that they all felt able to accept.

On Saturday afternoon she drove Steve and Kate to pick up Alice and Michael, and they went to the marina where Ben would be waiting.

It was a pleasant trip along the canal. Michael was a little surprised at first to see how much alike Kate and Jo were, and Alice was a little shy, not having a partner. But soon they were getting on well together. This time they had a full meal at the inn, and it was delicious. It was too cold to sit outside, but the interior was cosy and relaxing.

They were back at the marina quite early. Ben had arranged a taxi to take him to Manchester airport as his flight left at some unearthly hour of the morning. Alice didn't like keeping Michael up too late as he tired very easily. So they said their goodbyes on the narrow boat. Discreetly, the others left Jo some time alone with Ben.

'Will you miss me?' he asked.

'Desperately,' she teased. 'But a fortnight will be soon over. When you get back then, well, there's all sorts of things we can do.'

'All sorts of things,' he agreed. 'Jo, do you remember when we stopped for a sandwich on the way back from the conference in the Lakes? You told me never to tell you that I—'

She kissed him to stop him speaking. 'When you get back,' she said. 'By that time I will be genuinely, completely, absolutely cured. We can start again from the beginning.'

'If Rob lets us.'

'Rob will let us. Otherwise I shall ask for another opinion. I'm going to miss you, Ben.'

She knew she *would* miss him. But as she walked back to the car, her life seemed happier than it had in months. In a fortnight he'd be back.

She dropped off Alice first, Steve carrying the now fast asleep Michael into the house. Then she made for home. Steve would be staying the night, as he did on most Saturdays. Jo was very happy with this. No longer did Steve uncomfortably remind her of Harry.

'Let's all have a cocoa,' came Kate's sleepy voice. 'But since you've had nothing to drink, you can have a brandy in yours, Jo.'

'Sounds good,' said Jo. Cocoa with brandy in it was an idea Kate had brought back from America. It had seemed a bit excessive at first, but Jo had to admit it tasted gorgeous.

It took only ten minutes to reach her little estate and her own house. Headlights flashed across the front of the house as she turned into the drive, flashed across the front porch.

There was someone sitting on the front step.

Jo stamped on the brakes and the car stopped half in the road. She could see a shadowy figure stand up, and like a dream she saw half-remembered movements. It couldn't be! She had to be mistaken!

Now the man moved towards them. His face was

momentarily illuminated by the headlights, his eyes screwed up. 'It's Harry. Harry Russell,' Jo choked.

The car stalled, the headlights died. There was silence in the car. Jo didn't know what to say, what to do, what to think. Not two minutes before she had been so, so happy. And now...

Kate said, 'Steve, get out and get rid of him. He can go anywhere in the world, but he's not staying here.'

Through tear-blurred eyes Jo watched the two men meet. In the darkness it was hard to decide what was happening, and she could hear nothing. The two appeared to be arguing. Then Harry turned, waved at her and walked away. She remembered that wave. It gave her a shock, how well she remembered it.

Steve waited until Harry was long gone, and then got back in the car. 'He wants to talk to you,' he said to Jo. 'He says he's got to meet you, and if you won't meet him here he suggests the Royal Lancashire Hotel in town. He's staying there.'

'He's not coming here,' Jo cried. 'Never, never, never.'

'What did he want?' asked Kate.

Steve didn't speak for a while, and when he did his voice was thick. He reached out to rest his hand on Jo's shoulder. 'He says he made a mistake. Now he wants to put things right.'

Jo was speechless. She was hardly aware that Kate was easing her out of the car, leading her up the drive and into the house, that Steve was driving the car up into the garage. She sat in her front room, frozen to stillness, beyond thought.

Even Kate seemed to be unsure what to say—

though Jo could tell that she was incredibly angry. In the end it was Steve who made the decision. 'I'm Jo's GP,' he said. 'I'm going to give her a sedative and you can put her to bed. Is that OK, Jo?'

'Whatever you want,' she said.

Harry was back.

CHAPTER EIGHT

JO WOKE early, and lay in bed, worrying.

She had been looking forward to a quiet Sunday. A late breakfast with Kate and Steve, perhaps a walk over to see Michael and Alice in the afternoon. She would have missed Ben, even though he was coming back to her in a fortnight. But now her life was in turmoil again.

She realised Rob had been right. She wasn't cured of the harm Harry had done to her. It had been all right while Harry had been away—an almost legendary figure in Australia. Now he was here in Kirkhelen he was frighteningly real.

Who could she turn to for help? There was Kate, Steve or Andrew, of course, she wasn't short of friends. But the two who would be most use to help-ful—Rob and Ben—were both out of touch. She didn't know Rob's address in Switzerland. And Ben was now halfway across the Atlantic.

Kate came into her bedroom, carrying a mug of tea. She sat on the bed and took one of Jo's hands. 'You look dreadful,' she said with sisterly honesty.

'Thanks, Kate. I don't feel too good either.'

'I wish he'd never come back,' said Kate. 'You've been looking so happy recently. And now look what he's done to you.'

'Whatever it is, I'm doing it to myself.' Jo struggled upright and reached for her tea. 'I've been thinking about what to do, going over and over it in my mind. I think I'll have to meet him.'

'Why? Let me go down to the hotel and tell him to leave you alone.'

Jo shook her head. 'You know what he's like. If he's challenged he'll fight back. And, besides, it's something I've got to do. If I'm over him, then I should be able to see him.'

'You're still not completely over breaking your leg. That pulled you down an awful lot, kid.'

'I know. But—' Downstairs, the telephone rang.

They sat together in silence. The ringing stopped then they heard the rumble of Steve's voice. After a moment there was a tap on Jo's bedroom door. Steve came in, looking angry. 'That was him,' he said. 'He wants to talk to you. I said you were still asleep but that someone would phone back with an answer in an hour or so. He tried to say something more but I put down the phone. Jo, would you like me to go down and see him?'

'No!' Now she was beginning to feel rather angry. 'Thanks, anyway, but this is something I've got to do myself. I'm not running away from the likes of Harry Russell.'

'If you've got to see him then we'll all go down together,' said Kate. 'He can talk to all three of us.'

'He's a persuasive devil,' put in Steve.

It was an appealing suggestion. But it wouldn't do. The more Jo thought about it, the more she realised that she would never be free of Harry if she didn't face him herself. 'You can drive me down to the hotel,' she said, 'but I'm going to talk to him myself. I'd appreciate it if you waited for me, though.'

'We'll do that,' said Kate. 'Now, come downstairs and have some breakfast.'

The phone rang again fifteen minutes later when they were all sitting in the kitchen, eating toast. 'If that's him,' said Kate, 'he was told an hour.'

But it wasn't Harry. It was Eunice Price, some kind of cousin of Harry's. She had been invited to the wedding. She hadn't been in touch with Jo since Harry had left but now she wanted to speak to her.

'Harry's back, dear,' she said to Jo. 'Did you know that?'

'Yes, I knew,' said Jo.

'Poor dear, he's apparently had a breakdown, but he's nearly all right now. He's going to need help from all of us, isn't he? I was sorry to hear about the wedding, but I'm sure it'll all come out right in the end. Would you both like to pop round and see me some time?'

'No,' said Jo. 'Please, don't ring again. If there's anything I want I'll ask you.' Then she rang off. She knew what was happening. Harry was trying to mobilise his friends to pressure her.

'That was Eunice Price, suggesting I call round with Harry,' she said.

'Eunice Price!' Kate burst out laughing. 'She's the one who gave you the orange tablecloths as a wedding present, remember? I was glad to send them back.'

'They weren't exactly my taste,' Jo agreed.

'Neither was Eunice.'

Jo dressed carefully, took care with her make-up. Then she phoned the Royal Lancashire hotel and asked to speak to Harry Russell. Her hand wasn't trembling, she noticed, her hand wasn't trembling.

The sound of the familiar voice gave her butterflies. 'Good of you to call, Jo! How are you?'

'Very well, thank you. I'm enjoying work, I have my friends around me. What do you want?'

His voice was persuasive. 'Jo, we've got to meet and talk.'

'I've nothing to say to you. You've said it all. If it's about the house, get in touch with my solicitors.'

'I'm not interested in the house!' He sounded dismissive. 'I said you could keep it and I meant it.' His voice became more persuasive. 'Jo, I've been ill. I've made a monstrous mistake. Can we at least meet and talk about it? I could come up there and—'

'I don't want you to come near my house,' she interrupted. 'If you really have to see me I'll be down to the hotel in half an hour. We can have coffee in the lounge.'

'A bit public, don't you think? I thought we might have lunch somewhere. There's a lot we've got to—'

'I've got plans for the rest of the day. The hotel lounge in half an hour.' She rang off.

'How did it go?' asked Kate.

'All right. Well, I suppose all right so far.' Jo looked at herself in the hall mirror. Her face was white, her eyes shining, she looked under a strain. This was the last thing she needed to happen.

Steve and Kate drove her down to the hotel. 'We'll wait here in the car park,' Kate said. 'If you're not out in half an hour I'm coming in to fetch you. Remember he's a smooth operator.'

'My little sister protecting me again!' Jo was both amused and touched.

'Just remember to be on your guard,' said Kate.

Jo made the final adjustments to her make-up, took a deep breath and climbed out of the car.

Harry was in the hotel foyer, obviously waiting for her. He offered her his hand, and after a moment she took it. She couldn't speak. She peered at him, as if trying to make sense of what she saw. It was the same Harry Russell, of course, the man she had known so long. But somehow he was different. She was seeing him as if he were a stranger.

'Jo, good to see you.' He obviously didn't want to say much in the very public foyer. 'I've ordered coffee, I remember how you like it. Shall we go into the lounge? It's quiet there and we can talk.'

He led the way into the lounge and made for a corner, but she stopped in the middle of the room. 'This table will do,' she said. 'I'm not staying long.'

He sat down opposite her, managing not to show his irritation. A waitress who had been hovering came over, carrying the tray of coffee. As she put out the cups and silver pot, Jo had time to study Harry.

She realised she had been holding her breath. She had also been holding her emotions in check. Now she let them flood over her. What was she feeling, thinking?

Harry had changed. His hair was a little longer, his face thinner. His manner was more subdued. As ever, he was dressed smartly, if casually. He had always spent money on clothes. He was wearing well-cut dark trousers, a silk shirt and suede jacket. She was glad she had dressed smartly herself.

Jo couldn't think of anything to say. This man, who had hurt her so terribly, had been the centre of her life for eighteen months, had been all she'd thought about. Now what did he want?

He, too, was silent. He looked at her cautiously, as if not sure what to say.

She decided to speak first. 'What are you doing back here?' she asked abruptly. 'I thought you had a good job in Australia.'

He shrugged. 'The job didn't work out so my boss and I agreed to part on good terms. We didn't like each other's way of doing things.'

'So you're back here for good, then?'

'Yes, I'm looking for a job. I've got a couple of applications out.'

She couldn't help herself. 'So you had to leave in a hurry, again? Any Australian girl expected to miss you?'

'Jo, that's not fair, that's hurtful.' The reply flashed back, but his half-guilty expression made her wonder.

'You're wrong,' she told him, 'it's very fair. And nothing I could say to you Harry, could hurt you like you hurt me.'

Now he looked genuinely sad. 'Believe me, Jo, I'm sorry. More sorry than you can ever guess. I had everything with you and I threw it away. I must have been mad.'

'Not mad,' she told him, 'but completely, entirely selfish and cruel. What you did was unforgivable. Now, say what you have to say to me and then get out of my life.'

There was a silence. He looked thoroughly dejected. Then he said, 'May I just try to explain? I know you feel badly done by—you're entitled to. I'd just like you to try to understand a little. I'm entitled to that, aren't I?'

'You're entitled to nothing.'

She sipped her coffee, watched him as he stood, walked backwards and forwards, apparently agitated. Finally he dragged his seat round the table to be nearer to her and sat down again. 'Look, Jo, you're a nurse. I'm a doctor. We both know from time to time that people—the best-organised people—sometimes do things that are mad, irrational, completely out of character. That's what happened to me. Some kind of a brainstorm, I don't know why I did it. I had everything going for me—we had everything going for us.'

A monstrous suspicion was growing inside her. 'What are you trying to say, Harry?'

Before she could stop him he had grasped both her hands in his. 'Jo, I made the biggest mistake of my life. If you knew how I've regretted it. I'm not going to say any more now. But, please, there are things I've still got to say to you. We must meet again. And I hope in time you'll be able to forgive me. Then we'll see what we can make of our lives afterwards.'

She looked at him unbelievingly. 'You want me back,' she said. 'You must be mad. Never would I even dream of such a thing.'

She knew her voice was rising, but she didn't care. Dashing her cup into its saucer, she ran out of the building. Kate was talking to Steve and they didn't see her at first. Jo had a moment to register how happy they looked but that made her feel worse. Then they turned to see her tearful face. She saw Steve's concern, Kate's alarm and anger.

She pushed her way into the car and slammed the

door. 'I want to go home,' she said. 'Kate, he wants me back.'

'Over my dead body,' said Kate.

Straight after their lunch together Steve had to go into the surgery. He phoned Kate and Jo shortly after he arrived. 'Harry's just phoned me. He's saying that he's had some kind of a breakdown and that as a family member and a doctor I should be a bit supportive. I said that as a doctor I had seen no signs of a breakdown and I certainly didn't consider him any kind of a family member any more. He wasn't a happy man.'

Jo's nerves were jangling. She couldn't cope with this kind of tension. What would Harry do next? She knew that in spite of all the support she was getting, she was sliding back into the misery and lethargy she had felt when Harry had first left. Why couldn't Ben or Rob be here? The sight of either of them would do her so much good. But ultimately she had to cope with this herself.

'Sitting and moping like this is no good,' Kate said suddenly. 'Why don't you go and put on your jeans and a pair of boots?'

'Jeans and boots? What for?'

'Just do it. We're going off in the car.'

Kate drove her twenty miles or so to a place where the Pennines started their first push into the sky. There were gliders and parascenders above them. 'Now we walk,' said Kate, 'and we walk *hard*.' She led Jo up the nearest furze-bordered path.

For two hours they toiled onwards till their bodies hurt, the hair clung to their foreheads, their shirts stuck to their backs. Finally they came back to the park where they had left the car and bought a bottle of water each from a little kiosk.

'Feel better?' Kate asked.

'Well, yes. I think I do.' The physical suffering had taken Jo's mind off her other problems.

But when they got back to the house there was a letter waiting for her, hand-delivered. She recognised the flamboyant handwriting at once.

'Don't open it. Tear it up or burn it,' Kate urged. 'Or let me take it back to him unopened.'

'No. I can't keep on avoiding things, I have to face them. Remember, he's very persistent.'

Her heart was pounding as it had been on the walk she had just finished. But this was different. She went upstairs to shower, then felt better. She tried to compose herself and opened the letter.

Dear Jo,

I've been watching the house, and waiting till you've gone out before delivering this letter. I realise you don't want to see me again—well, not straight away—and I'm finding this difficult myself.

First, once again I'm sorry for what I did to you. You are right, what I did was unforgivable. If you only knew how the knowledge of this has made me suffer, you might even feel a little sympathy for me.

But I want to make things up. I know I've got no right to ask or say anything, but I want you back. I want things to be as they were before. I suspect they never can be, but if we both try, our relationship could be strengthened by what has passed.

I want you to balance two things. First, the happiness of the eighteen months that we spent with each other. Those were the happiest days of my life, I suspect the happiest days of your life, too. Now set those times against just one day when I had a brainstorm. I've thought of you every day since I arrived in Australia. I've been haunted by you.

It might be hard for you to forgive me, but let me meet you again to see if there is anything left of our feelings for each other. Please, please think of happier times. We could have them again.

I love you. Harry.

'He writes a good letter, I'll give him that,' Kate said when she had looked through it. 'Of course, it's all rubbish and he probably copied it out of a magazine. Shall I tear it up?'

'No,' Jo said listlessly. 'I'm going to read through it again.'

'You don't believe any of it, do you? You're not thinking of going back to him, are you?'

'No, of course not. But I just can't refuse to see him. I've got to be able to see him face to face. If I didn't I'd be afraid of meeting him every time I went out. I've got to get on top of this, little sister.'

Kate came over to hug her. 'You can and you will. We Wildes are a tough bunch.'

Jo was discussing the theatre lists for the next week when Andrew said suddenly, 'I understand Harry Russell is on the scene again. Have you seen him?'

'Yes, he's been in touch.' She knew she could rely on Andrew to be discreet. 'He says he wants to get back together again. Says what happened was because he had a brainstorm.'

'I've forgotten more about what he calls brainstorms than that man will ever know. In fact, they don't exist. He's talking total rot. You're not paying any attention to him, are you?'

'We spent a lot of time together, Andrew.'

'You'd be a fool if you spent any more with him. Still, you know your own business. I take it Ben doesn't know anything about this?'

'He's in Philadelphia, Andrew. I'm not going to bother him while he's over there. And Rob Simpson is lost on a course somewhere in Switzerland.'

'You've got problems,' Andrew grunted. 'But remember, problems need to be shared to be resolved. Now, this next case…'

When she got home that night there was an immense bunch of expensive flowers waiting for her. 'I thought you might like to have a glance before I throw them onto the compost heap,' said Kate.

'Just a glance,' said Jo. She took the card from the centre of the bouquet. It read, 'all my love, Harry.' Angrily she tore up the card. Would he never learn? 'You can throw them on the compost heap now,' she said to Kate.

At eight the phone rang. Kate was out. 'Jo, please, don't ring off, it's Harry. It's OK to phone you, isn't it?'

'What do you want?'

'Just a chat. Did you get the flowers?'

'Yes. I threw them out. You wasted your money.'

'Ah.'

'Why did you think I might want anything from you?'

'I just wanted to give you something. Have you been thinking about what I said?'

'No, there's absolutely no need to think. You did something absolutely unforgivable. I'm not going to forgive you. I want you out of my life.'

'You can't put me out of your life. I'll always be a part of it. We have memories, happy memories. They're as much a part of you as they are of me. Remember that picnic in the woods?'

Just for a moment she did remember, though previously she had half forgotten. It had been a warm day, they had carried a basket of food deep into the woods and had sat on a blanket by a stream. Both had been working hard. They hadn't wanted much to do with anything, just to be by each other. She had loved him then.

To her horror, the emotions she had experienced at the picnic flashed over her again. Then they were gone, leaving her feeling sick and apprehensive.

'I just don't want to hear from you again,' she said, knowing she had been betrayed by her own feelings.

'I think you do,' he said quickly. Had he perhaps detected her uncertainty? How could he have? He went on, 'Look, I'm coming into the hospital tomorrow to see a few friends. How about I meet you for lunch?'

'No! I don't want to be seen with you.'

'Then I'll meet you somewhere afterwards. It doesn't have to be at work. Come on, you owe me that much because of the times we've had. And I need your help, Jo.'

She didn't know why but she found herself agreeing to meet him—not the next day but Wednesday night.

Just for half an hour. 'And listen. If you even try to speak to me tomorrow in the hospital, I'll cancel. But I'll meet you at the Royal Lancaster on Wednesday at six.'

'But I'd rather take you to—'

'For half an hour at six on Wednesday.' She rang off.

When she got back home there was a message from Ben on the answering machine. 'Working hard, learning a lot but missing you no end. Love you, Ben.' It brought home to her how much she was missing him. Life with Ben was fun. There was always something to laugh at, something they could enjoy together. She relaxed with Ben. By contrast, her nerves in the past three days had been stretched tighter than steel springs. How she wished he was there!

She had a restless night, and when she awoke her leg ached. She was still doing her exercises. Life could be very unfair.

When she went to the hotel at five past six on Wednesday, she was in an aggressive mood. She wasn't sure how to deal with Harry. 'What d'you want?' she asked abruptly. 'I haven't much time.'

He didn't snap back, but looked hurt. 'Here, I've brought these to remind you of happier times.' He led her to a table, then spread out a handful of photographs. She recognised them as being from various trips they had taken together.

'I've seen all these. In fact, you gave me copies of most. What about them?'

'Of course, I forgot. You'll have your own copies.'

'Not any more. I burned every photograph with you on.'

But she flicked through the pictures as he talked of happier times. 'Here, remember when we went up to Ambleside? This is the picture we took from the steamer. And here's that peculiar car ferry, with the cables coming up out of the water. Happy days, Jo.'

They had been happy days. That was the problem. Suddenly she got angry and pushed the pictures together into a pile. A couple of them fell to the floor. 'I'm not interested in your holiday snaps,' she said roughly. 'I would have liked to look at pictures taken at my wedding. But because of you there aren't any.'

'Jo, I'm sorry! How many times do I have to say it? We'd known each other for two years. Now, was it like me? Be honest, was that the kind of behaviour you expected from me? You'd known me long enough.'

There was a silence. 'Well, it was a shock,' she said.

'So I'm asking you to have a little understanding. Just try to be me for a while.'

'I'd rather not. And I'm going now.'

Harry stood when she did. 'Jo, I think we've got somewhere this evening. When can I see you again? I know you think you don't want to, and it'll take time, but I don't mind waiting. Shall I phone you tomorrow night? Say about nine? Or I could call round if you like.'

'Don't do that. Kate might go for you with the carving knife. And she'd be entitled to.'

'All right, so I'll phone. Tomorrow at nine. I'm looking forward to it.'

Only when she got outside did Jo realise just how cleverly she'd been manipulated.

*   *   *

The next two days were a blur. Jo took no interest in anything. She appeared to be losing her ability to think. Harry did phone on Thursday night. At first he talked generally about his early life in Kirkhelen, about how he and Steve had been very close and that he hoped they would get that way again. 'I've talked to him again, Jo. He's more sympathetic now, he understands what I've been through.'

Jo wondered about this, but only vaguely. Harry was subjecting her to a constant, soft battering, and she couldn't cope with it. He did most of the talking. When he finally rang off she realised she'd promised to meet him again on Saturday. He would come round. What was happening to her?

On Friday morning she called round to see the consultant who had set her leg. Without telling him there was a specific reason, she told him about her lethargy, her inability to think. 'I'll suggest a tonic of some sort. I'll be in touch with your GP. Don't forget, you had considerable damage to your leg. It's bound to affect your general health, possibly for weeks to come. I take it you don't want some time off work?'

'That's the last thing I want. Work is keeping me sane.'

'I thought so. Don't be too worried about this, Jo. As my old friend Andrew is always saying, the mind and the body are interconnected.'

This man was also the consultant for whom Harry had worked. 'I hear Harry Russell is around.' he said carefully. 'I hope he doesn't apply for a job here again, he won't get one.'

'You wouldn't employ him?'

'Between one hospital worker and another, he

wasn't a bad orthopaedic surgeon. But he was too fond of himself, too reliant on his own judgement, and not ready enough to listen to anyone else's. Harry could never believe that it was possible that he was wrong. So much confidence is dangerous.'

Jo was thoroughly confused. She just didn't know what to think.

Saturday morning. Kate had said that she wanted to be in the house when Harry came, she had a few words to say to him herself. Somehow Jo had persuaded her that that wasn't a good idea. So Kate had left early, apparently to stay with Steve. Jo was rather surprised at the ease with which she'd been persuaded to go. But her sister had always been unpredictable.

Jo stayed in bed until they had gone then got up and made herself a mug of coffee that she didn't much want. Listlessly she wandered round the house in her dressing-gown. Harry was coming. He had an important appointment in Liverpool and he didn't know when it would finish but it should be some time between twelve and two. Another pointless session, another period of half listening to those smooth, carefully marshalled arguments.

The doorbell rang. It was eleven o'clock. Harry couldn't come this early, this was ludicrous! A faint anger touched her apathy. Pulling her gown round her, she went to the front door. He could just go away and return when—

On the doorstep was Ben.

She couldn't believe it. It was Ben. His clothes looked rumpled, there were lines of fatigue round his eyes, a travelling case leaned against his leg. But it was Ben. With a sob she threw herself into his arms. 'Ben, Ben, it's so good to see you.'

Somehow he moved her back into the hall and closed the door behind them. She didn't want to let go of him. From him she could draw comfort. If Ben was here everything would soon be all right. She could feel the familiar solidity of his muscular chest, smell the cologne that he used. It must have been a while since he'd been able to shave, his cheek was rough against hers. And she loved it.

She lifted her head, caught a glimpse of herself in the hall mirror. She looked a wreck! Hair a mess, eyes red. She couldn't talk to Ben looking like this!

Hastily she stepped back, pushing her hair out of her eyes. Her mug of coffee was on the hall table. She took it and thrust it at him. 'Please, Ben, drink this and sit down just for five minutes. I need five minutes, that's all. I don't want to talk to you looking like this.'

'You look beautiful to me,' he said.

'I'm not beautiful! Ben, please, I want five minutes. Oh, I'm so glad to see you!'

She left him sitting in the kitchen and rushed upstairs. She managed to shower, brush her hair, pull on fresh underwear and trousers and a clean shirt. A minimal touch of make-up. And all in, well, eight minutes. Now much more self-assured, she ran downstairs. She felt like a human being again.

He had finished her mug of coffee so she put on the percolator to make him more and slid two pieces of bread into the toaster. 'I'll do you breakfast,' she said. 'You look as if you need it.' She was confident now, resourceful.

Then she sat at the table and took his hands. 'You

can go and have a bath later,' she said. 'I know you'll feel like one. But first there are things you have to tell me. Why are you back so soon? I thought the course had another week to run.'

'It does. But Andrew's taking my place. We talked it over with the course director, it'll work out quite well.'

'Andrew! What's he doing in America?'

'He's taking my place, that's all. He thought I was needed back in England. He phoned me and said he was worried about you. Apparently your fiancé is back.'

'He's not my fiancé! We were engaged once but he's not my fiancé!'

'I thought not. Anyway, Andrew isn't a fan of Harry. He said if he had rat poison, he'd use it on the man. He thinks that Harry is having an undue influence on you and he thought I could stop it.'

Jo thought about this. 'So he arranged to fly to America and take your place so you could come and look after me?'

'More or less, yes,' Ben said.

That took some getting used to. 'Why—how did he know I needed some…help?' she asked.

'Well, of course, he knew about Harry's arrival and he got the impression from talking to you that you weren't very happy about it. He said your work in Theatre was as good as it had ever been, but you weren't yourself. He's a doctor, don't forget, he can tell when something's wrong. And it doesn't have to be something physical. He wanted to get in touch with Rob Simpson, but that proved impossible.' Ben paused for a moment. 'He thought you might do something foolish.'

'Like going back to Harry? Ben, there's no chance! That's the last thing I want to do. And I'm going to be all right now, all right now you're back. You can help me, tell me what to do.'

Ben fiddled with his cup. 'Jo, I tried to help you once before. I did the best job I could because I wanted to help. But Rob had to take over. You know what he said, that it was possible you'd fallen for me because I was your counsellor. Neither of us want that kind of relationship and—'

'Ben, Rob was wrong! I fell in love with you because…because you're the most lovable man I've ever met. Not for any other reason. And now you've got to help me.'

He put his arms round her and for a while she rested with her head on his chest, happy, knowing that all would be well now.

After five minutes she became aware of the tempting smell of toast. She'd forgotten she'd promised him breakfast!

'What do you want on your toast?' she asked. 'Would you like an egg or some bacon?' She had to look after her man.

'Just butter, if that's OK,' he said. 'Jo, when are you seeing this man again?'

'He's coming some time after twelve. Ben, I want you to stay here and help me with him.'

'No,' said Ben.

She looked at him incredulously. 'Ben, I've told you, I need help with this man. You've got to tell me what to do. He keeps going on about how good things used to be—and I suppose some of them were. He shows me photographs of us together, and says it wasn't his fault he cancelled the wedding, he had a brainstorm, he was ill. He's…very insistent, Ben, but I don't want him back.'

Ben stood to take her in his arms again, and as she felt his body against hers she felt certain that she had never loved him as she did now. He was tired, his suit was bedraggled, but she loved him.

His next words came as a shock. 'Jo, I can't help you. You must see, this is something that you must do for yourself. Rob says that it's always wrong to advise people, they must make up their own minds.'

'But what do *you* want for me?' she asked.

'You know that very well. Above all, I want you to be happy. But only you can decide where that happiness comes from. You know that Rob suggested that we remain friends but…stay apart a while? That's been a strain for me, Jo. But in no way will I take advantage of you, force you to do something that I want and perhaps you don't. You must be certain in your own mind. You must make your own decisions. Is that fair?'

'Yes,' she said quietly after a while. 'That's fair. Will you stay here when he comes?'

'I don't think that's a good idea. You say he's coming today, some time after twelve?'

She shrugged. 'It could be any time in the next two hours. It'd be like him to come early.'

'Then I'll go now. Jo, you know this is the hardest thing I've ever done in my life?'

She thought about it a moment, looked at his

stricken face. 'Yes, I know that,' she said. 'But before you go just hug me again.'

He held her, and she tried to draw power from his body, know that he could be hers. If she had the strength to claim him.

'I'm technically on call since Andrew is away,' he told her. 'I ought to report into the hospital. But can I call you this afternoon? After he…when you have…'

'You can call me at any time,' she said. 'Ben, I love you.'

'And I love you, Jo,' he replied.

He left then. I didn't even make him breakfast, she thought to herself. She didn't think to wonder how he would get to the hospital.

CHAPTER NINE

STEVE was waiting for Ben in his car, parked well away from the house. The two men had become firm friends. Andrew had phoned Steve, telling him what he proposed to do, and Steve had volunteered to pick Ben up from the airport. Kate was waiting impatiently at Steve's surgery.

'How did it go?' asked Steve.

Ben shrugged. 'Not too well. She's showing some of the classic signs of low-grade depression but I don't think it's that. Has this Harry got that much of a hold over her? Could he be serious? You know the man best.'

Steve sighed. 'He's my cousin and I've known him all my life. I liked him once, he's a very likeable man. A bit slap-happy in his medicine perhaps, but more or less conscientious. The trouble with Harry is that he's nearly always got his own way. So now he thinks that's what he's entitled to. And he could sell fridges to Eskimos.'

'That's what I thought.'

'I hope you told her that you loved her,' Steve said. 'That's why we brought you back to England.'

'I told her I loved her. But she knew that already.'

'So are you going back to the house to help her when she meets Harry?'

'No,' Ben said flatly, 'I daren't.'

'You daren't? Ben, she needs help. She can't meet

that man on her own—he'll wear her down just by talking. And she's not strong right now. You said so yourself.'

Ben lifted his shoulders in defeat. 'I just daren't stay and help her with him, though God knows I was tempted. But this is something she must do herself. She must get rid of Harry because she wants to, not because I'm an alternative.'

Steve was silent for a moment, then he said, 'I hope you know what you're doing. There's no one I would rather have as an in-law than you. And I hope Jo is all right. Now, shall I drop you off at the narrow boat?'

'No, I'd better sign in at the hospital. I can have a shower there and I'll change into scrubs. I'll look at my mail first and see how things are going. Then I'll phone Jo in a couple of hours.'

'Whatever you think best. Be in touch when you have some news.'

In some ways it was good to get back into the routine of hospital life. Ben dictated the replies to a few letters, looked through the case notes of the most recent admittances.

There were a couple of minor queries from one of the house officers. He bleeped her, then went onto the ward to look at a patient with her. Mrs Coulter had had a clot removed. Now she was under observation and the house officer felt her vital signs were getting low.

Ben looked at the observations, conducted a quick examination himself and then decided that there was little to worry about.

'You were right to call me,' he said, 'but I don't think this is too serious. Remember, there's often no absolutely certain diagnosis. As I said, you were right to be worried, but experience tells me that this condition isn't dangerous. But I could be wrong, so keep an eye on Mrs Coulter here. OK?'

'OK,' said the house officer. 'Er, thanks for the help.'

'It's what I'm here for,' said Ben.

He enjoyed this casual teaching. As he went back to his office it struck him that what he had just said to the house officer applied to his own case. There was no absolutely certain diagnosis in the case of him and Jo. Had he done the right thing? All he could say was that he had done the best as he saw it, and not given in to his own personal feelings. This is *about* your own personal feelings, a nasty voice inside him rasped. Perhaps he should have given in.

The phone rang as he entered his office. Irritated, he lifted it. 'Yes?' he snapped.

Jo didn't know how she felt. Never had she been so dissatisfied with life. There was a warm glow at the thought of the trouble Andrew had gone to for her, and a thrill of anticipation at the knowledge that Ben was home again. But she needed more. All right, so Ben had said that he loved her. Why then wouldn't he help her face Harry?

On the other hand, she had to admire what he was trying to do. He wanted to be an honourable man. Distractedly, she started to clear away dishes in the kitchen. Ben hadn't even stayed for his toast.

The doorbell rang. This time it was certain to be Harry. It was. She opened the door. He was there, smiling, as well dressed as ever, a large bunch of flowers in his arms. As he entered he tried to kiss her, though not too hard. She offered him her cheek. He didn't press her, he was good that way.

'I remember this house so well,' he said as he came through into the kitchen. 'I remember picking those curtains. We had to visit six different stores before you could find the ones that matched the wall colour.'

'As I remember, I made most of the choices,' she said. 'You just wanted to get things done as quickly as possible.'

'I had every confidence in your taste. Where shall I put these flowers?'

'Drop them in the sink for now,' she said indifferently.

Without being asked, he took a seat at the kitchen table. It was the seat where Ben had sat and she felt more irritated than ever. 'You couldn't make me a coffee, could you?' he asked. 'I haven't had a drink all morning, I've been for a preliminary meeting in Liverpool. There might be a job for me there.' He took some papers from inside his jacket and threw them on the table. 'It'd mean a small drop in salary but I wouldn't mind that because it would be local—near you. I could even commute from here every day.'

'Don't include me in your plans,' Jo said. 'You play no part in mine.' Then, because there was no reason not to, she started to make him a coffee.

He looked at her in surprise. 'I thought we were getting somewhere. I always found you an understanding compassionate person. No one blamed you for breaking your leg, why should you blame me for some kind of mental aberration? Because you know that's

what it was. Up to that terrible day, did you ever think
that that was the kind of person I was?'

No, she hadn't. And the shock had been so great.
'What other women have you been seeing while
you've been away?' she asked.

'None. I swear, not one.' Perhaps his answer was a
little too slick. But she didn't know, she just couldn't
tell.

He went on, 'I've thought of no other woman. All
I thought about was you.'

'I've been seeing someone,' she said. 'I've got very
fond of him. He's called Ben Franklin, he's our new
registrar.'

Harry was clever. He didn't seem angry, upset.
Instead, he was sympathetic. 'It's understandable. You
were hurt, you reached out, he offered you some comfort. But can you compare a couple of months with
this man—when you know you were actively miserable—with the two years of happiness that we had
together?'

Put that way, it sounded reasonable. It wasn't, of
course, but it sounded that way. Remorselessly, he
went on. 'I'm not suggesting that we do anything sudden, Jo. Just that we keep our options open. It'll take
a long time before you can forgive me, I understand
that. But if we see each other occasionally, if you
come to realise that…'

He was going on. On and on and on. It was like a
current sweeping her out to sea. No matter how she
struggled, no matter what progress she made, the current was still there.

The front doorbell rang. Not once, but several times,
with the urgency of someone who intended to come

in no matter what. There was a loud rapping, too. Someone was definitely in a hurry.

'Who the devil can that be?' Harry was displeased. He didn't like being interrupted. Jo shrugged and went to open the door.

There was Ben.

He was dressed in his greens and he wasn't smiling. But she didn't care. She looked at him and she was happy. 'Ben, come on in. Come and meet Harry.'

She thought Ben had changed his mind, had come to be with her when she faced Harry to give her strength. She was glad.

Ben walked into the kitchen, gave a curt nod to Harry then ignored him.

'You're needed at the hospital,' he said to Jo. 'You're needed right now. You've got to scrub for me. This is an emergency and I need all the help I can get.'

Jo was instantly alert. 'What sort of emergency?'

'It's Michael. When he woke this morning he complained of a headache. After breakfast he vomited violently and complained he couldn't see very well. Then he got very sleepy, and at that stage Alice phoned for an ambulance. My junior registrar checked his notes, gave him a CT scan at once and—'

Jo had seen enough cases to guess what had happened. 'He's haemorrhaging into the brain.'

'That's right. We've got to get in there and at least drain it or he'll die. We knew this could happen but we hoped to have more time.'

'But, Ben, should you operate? First of all, he's family. Secondly, you're not fit. You've just flown in from America, you shouldn't do anything like this for at least twenty-four hours.'

'I know. I've phoned Liverpool and everywhere else where there might be a good surgeon available. There just isn't one. I'm Michael's best chance.'

She looked at him. There were signs of fatigue in his face but he was calmly confident. This boy needed his professional skills and he should have them.

'OK, if you can operate I can scrub,' she said. 'When do we start?'

'He's getting prepped now. I've laid on an anaesthetist. Michael's already on a ventilator, he's already having difficulty breathing. I'd like to start in half an hour—this is going to take quite some time.'

Harry chose this moment to intervene. Afterwards Jo thought that he couldn't have picked a worse time. 'Just a minute,' he said. 'Jo's not on duty and she's not on call. Now, we're having rather an important discussion here so if you don't mind we'd like to—'

'Off you go, Harry,' Jo interrupted briskly. 'I'm busy now with something that is far more important than anything you can possibly have to say.'

Harry didn't like rejection and he didn't expect it either—she could tell by his face. He was annoyed. 'But, Jo…' he spluttered.

Now she could see the two men side by side. Harry was definitely the better looking and he had taken such obvious care with his expensive casual clothes. But his appearance was sulky, he wasn't getting his own way. Ben was looking tired, his hair was a mess and he was wearing hospital greens, possibly the least sexy clothing ever. But to Jo he was wonderful. There was something solid and satisfying about him. This was a man she could love. And at this very moment all her last feelings for Harry died. She was free of him and of her past with him.

'Harry, can't you tell this is important?' she said, as if addressing a child. 'Now, off you go, and I'll give you a call some time next week. Please don't ring me, I'll be busy.'

He had been dismissed. His power over her had gone. She could tell from his face that he knew it, and he didn't like it. Without another word he turned and left the room. They heard the slam of the front door.

Ben leaned over and kissed her swiftly on the lips. 'When you have to be, you're tough, aren't you?' he said. 'I like it. Come on, we've got to get to the hospital.'

Once there, first she went to the anteroom to the theatre where Alice was bent over her unconscious son. She gave her friend a hug, told her that they would do everything in their power for Michael. She knew that once in Theatre there would be no time for feelings, emotions. The operating team would have to concentrate solely on the task in hand. Poor Alice would have the worst of it, she could do nothing but wait and pray.

Jo had time for the swiftest of showers and scrubbed up before dressing in greens and moving to the Theatre. Much of her work was done before the surgeons arrived. She checked that all was well with the trolley, that the others in the theatre knew what was to happen.

The anaesthetist came in with Michael and a male nurse, and they carefully placed the patient in the sitting position. For a craniotomy, this was the best position, but there was a danger that blood would drain down the body so Michael was wearing a pressure suit to combat this. Ben took his position in a high chair behind Michael. The anaesthetist was to one side, Jo to the other.

All of them wore caps and masks, of course. But as Jo looked at Ben, she felt that he could tell just from her eyes what she was feeling. Certainly, she knew what he was feeling.

There were others present, of course. Students had to learn. There was the junior registrar who had been so quick to give Michael a CT scan, a junior and a senior house officer.

Ben said, 'The patient isn't particularly strong, but we have to operate to stop the haemorrhage in the midbrain. Pressure from the blood is affecting visual and motor functions.' He pointed to the results of the CT scan pinned to the theatre wall. Then, without looking, he stretched out his hand and Jo placed the scalpel in it.

To begin with, the operation was straightforward. Ben cut down to the skull, drilled and then cut out a flap of bone. Quickly he cut through the triple membrane that protected the brain. Jo was at hand, passing him the high-frequency electric diathermy needle to seal off the smaller blood vessels and clamps to hold back the larger ones.

Now came the crux. Slowly Ben dissected downwards, making his way towards the midbrain. Here he was on his own. No one but he could make these decisions.

'Cardiac arrest!' For the first time the anaesthetist spoke. Michael's heart had stopped beating. Jo saw that Ben looked up and then continued with his work. This was nothing to do with him. From the corner of her eye Jo saw the anaesthetist working with controlled expertise, pumping increased oxygen into Michael, injecting adrenaline through the IV access, giving him more blood. After a few desperate seconds the anaesthetist said, 'Heart beating again.' Ben worked on.

The tumour in Michael's brain had pressed against a blood vessel and split it. Unfortunately, as chemotherapy had reduced the size of the tumour, the ruptured blood vessel had leaked into the brain. Ben couldn't just drain the area. The blood vessel would have to be clipped.

Working in the tiniest of spaces, Ben did what he could. He didn't speak now, no one but he could see what was happening. Then finally he said, 'I think we've got it. We can close now.'

No one in the theatre spoke. But Jo could feel the hope spreading through the team.

Outside the theatre Ben stripped off his blood-covered gloves and pulled down his mask. He smiled at Jo. 'That was something I never want to repeat,' he said. 'But we did it. Do you want to come and speak to Alice before we change?'

'Very much so.'

The post-op nurse and the anaesthetist were still working on Michael and Alice surveyed them fearfully from the other side of the room. Jo could guess what she was thinking. The array of tubes, the masses of equipment seemed to dwarf the small body of the child they were trying to keep alive.

'It all went quite well, Alice,' Ben said. 'As I told

you before, this was a very serious operation. But it went quite well, and I think you should be, well, reasonably hopeful.'

'He's going to get better, isn't he, Ben?' Alice's voice was shaking.

Jo's heart went out to Alice. She knew that all the woman wanted was reassurance. But Ben knew better than to give any kind of unconditional guarantee. The team had done what they could, and Michael now had a fighting chance. But now he would have to fight on his own.

'I think there's a good chance he will get better,' Ben said gently, 'but it was a very serious operation. All we can do now is wait and pray. Now Michael's going to be specialled for a while—that means that someone will be with him all the time. I've arranged for you to have a bedroom next to his room. You can spend as much time with him as you want. But I suggest you get some sleep. Michael's not going to wake up properly for quite some time. I'm going to be on call but right now I need some sleep myself.'

'That you for what you both have done,' Alice said.

Ben and Jo went to the rooms where they could shower and change. 'You don't have to sleep in hospital,' Jo said when they met afterwards. 'You can bring your mobile in case you're needed here and sleep at my house. Kate is out till later.'

'I'd like that,' he said after a pause.

It was early evening as they walked out of the hospital. The sun was low in the sky and there was still a little warmth in the air. It felt good to be out. 'I've been cooped up too much recently,' Ben said, 'first the plane and then the theatre. Too much artificial light. It's good to get out.'

'Will you take me on the narrow boat again soon?'

'I'd love to. But not right now.' He swayed slightly as he bent to open the car door.

'Why don't I drive?' she asked. 'You're tired.'

'And that's another good idea.'

She liked it that he was happy to have her drive his car.

'Are you hungry?' she asked as they negotiated the little town centre.

The question seemed to surprise him.

'Yes, I am,' he said after a moment's thought. 'Do you know, I hadn't realised it.'

'I could show you what a wonder housewife I am and knock us up something from the odd bits left in the fridge. But I've got a better idea. You do like Chinese food, don't you?'

'Just so long as there's rice with it.'

So she drove him to Mr Ho's and went in and asked for a banquet for two as Ben dozed outside. Mr Ho's banquet was known to most people in town, and certainly to everyone in the hospital. 'You'll like this,' she said as she got back in the car, carrying a wonderful smelling carrier bag.

A little later they were sitting in Jo's kitchen, opening a variety of foil-wrapped cartons. 'Do you want wine?'

Ben shook his head. 'There's still the offchance that I might be called back to hospital. But I'd like a chilled beer if you've one.' So they had a lager each.

The meal was fantastic. After chicken and corn soup there were prawn crackers, fried rice, beef, chicken, pork and vegetables in a variety of sauces and then toffee apples to finish. They couldn't finish everything and at the end they both felt better. 'That was really good,' he said.

He finished his beer as she quickly cleared away, mostly a question of throwing cartons into the bin.

'I'm trying to stay awake until my normal bedtime,' he said. 'If I aim for ten o'clock, that gives us one and a half hours first. We can talk.'

'Talk as in chat? Are you going to tell me about the course you've been on, and how you liked Philadelphia?'

'No. Talk as in talk. About me and you. And perhaps about Harry.'

Jo saw him watching her and guessed he was wondering how she would take this. She didn't mind. 'Sounds like serious stuff, then,' she said. 'Go and sit in the lounge and I'll bring us both a cup of tea.'

When she carried the tray through Ben was sitting on the couch. He lifted an arm companionably. She put down the tray and sat beside him, leaning against his chest. Then she kicked off her slippers and ran her bare feet up and down his leg.

'We can deal with Harry at once,' she said. 'He was something to me once, but I know he's nothing now. There's no doubt at all in my mind. Harry has gone.'

'I thought so. That leaves us two to consider.'

'Drink your tea,' she said, feeling just a little apprehensive. She had a sense that things were about to change, that after this evening her life might be different. What was he going to say?

'Look, I'm tired,' he said. 'It was a hard course, I had the plane journey and then the operation took it out of me. I know what I ought to do is just loll here, holding you and feeling you and smelling you and being blissfully happy.'

'Sounds a good plan to me.'

'And I might fall asleep at any moment.'

'There's a double bed upstairs. I'll even let you choose the side you want to sleep on. Kate and Steve won't be here till past midnight.'

'Don't tempt me, you wanton woman. I told you, I have things to say.' He paused and drank more tea. 'When I met you first, you were engaged to someone else. Very kindly, because we were to work on the same team, you invited me to the wedding. I was really looking forward to working with you. And because you were about to be married it was quite impossible to think of you as a very attractive woman. You were to be a colleague, perhaps a friend. Nothing more was possible. I had to keep on telling myself that.'

She pushed herself up from the couch so she could look at him full in the face, surprised and not a little delighted. 'Ben! You fancied me at once!'

'You bet I fancied you,' he growled. 'You were the most attractive woman I had ever met. You had everything—appearance, voice, brains. You were just a gorgeous woman. Then things went badly wrong for you, you broke your leg and no way could I even hint at what I felt. And honestly, Jo, when I said that I wanted to help, when I said I wanted to be a friend, I meant it.'

'I remember you saying how much you despised people who took advantage of those who were vulnerable,' she said slowly. 'I admired you for that. Did it hurt you to say that all you wanted was to be a friend to me?'

'It could have done,' he acknowledged, 'but I was trying to help. I believe that friendship should always come before love. But anyway…things developed. At Coniston I made love to—'

'No, you did not! We made love together. Don't ever forget that, it's important.'

He leaned over to kiss her. 'All right, we did something together and, whatever it was, it was marvellous. But then there was Rob, suggesting I might have taken advantage of you. That you might feel nothing for me, that it was *transference*.' He seemed to spit out the word.

'I like Rob,' she said. 'I like him no end. And I know he helped me a lot. But he was wrong about you and me. I did nothing I didn't want to.'

'Good. Now, if you're certain that you've got Harry out of your system, we'll never mention the name again.'

'I'm more than certain he's out of my system. But don't say we'll never mention him. He was part of my life, I've got to accept that.' Anxiously she asked, 'Can you live with that? I don't want any ghosts to come between us.'

'Oh, yes, I can live with that. After all, I've got you now.'

It was very comfortable just lying there with her head on his shoulder, feeling him breathing, the gentle rise and fall of his chest under her cheek. For a while neither of them said anything, both perfectly happy. Then Jo pushed Ben gently.

'You might as well sleep in a bed as here,' she said. 'Come on, you'll rest better there.'

He opened his eyes and blinked. 'It sounds like a good idea.' Then he shook his head and said, 'I fell asleep and I had something important to say to you.'

'Something important? Mmm? I wonder what that could be.'

'Jo, I love you. Will you marry me?'

'What?' She jerked upright. 'Ben Franklin, you fall asleep on my couch, just wake up in time to remember that there's something you've forgotten—and then ask me to marry you. What kind of a romantic proposal is that?'

'It might not be very romantic,' he said judiciously, 'but it's very sincere. I've wanted to marry you for weeks. I've just been prevented from asking you. I even went into a jeweller's shop and looked at rings. We'll have to go back together. Like I said, I love you, Jo, and I want to marry you.'

'Are you going to go to sleep before I give you an answer?' she asked reproachfully.

'It's possible if you don't do it soon,' he admitted. 'All my feelings are mixed up. I'm so tired I can hardly face walking upstairs to go to bed. I feel vaguely pleased with the operation on Michael—that was a good bit of work from both of us. And over all there's the idea that I love you and that without you life will be grey. I want to spend all my time with you, work, play and sleep with you. *Will* you marry me, Jo?'

'Of course I will. I love you and I think you've known for weeks that I'll marry you. Now, will you come here and kiss me before you fall into a coma?'

'Oh, yes,' he said.

He kissed her. Then he kissed her again, much harder this time, and— 'No,' she said firmly. 'We'll do that when I can be certain that you'll be able to stay awake.'

'So much for my masculine pride.'

'Well, there's always tomorrow morning. Now, come upstairs and get undressed.'

'That's what I'm supposed to say,' he mumbled.

Jo couldn't sleep, she was too excited. She sat up in bed, reading, the bedside light carefully directed so that it didn't disturb Ben. Not that anything could. He was well and truly asleep.

She had phoned the hospital and talked to the nurse who was specialling Michael. He was doing well, the nurse said, there was absolutely no cause for alarm. Alice had sat by her son until the nurse had coaxed her to bed.

Jo felt blissfully happy. There was the warmth of Ben's body reaching out to her, a naked arm trailing over the covers. There was the sound of his heavy breathing. She leaned over to kiss the arm. What more could she want?

From downstairs she heard the noise of doors being carefully opened. Kate and Steve were back. She had to tell someone. Without disturbing Ben, she slipped out of bed, pulled on her gown over her nightie and went downstairs. Kate and Steve were in the kitchen, drinking tea.

'Did I see Ben's car outside?' Steve asked mischievously.

Kate looked at her sister. 'There's a look in your eye,' she said. 'You've got something to tell us, haven't you?'

'I'm an engaged woman,' said Jo.

EPILOGUE

THEY picked the ring together, at the same little jeweller's shop Ben had visited before. The lady assistant couldn't have been more helpful. Together they chose a sapphire of the deepest blue, surrounded by diamonds. 'Do come back to see us when you want a wedding band.' The assistant beamed.

And a week later Steve and Kate invited Jo and Ben to dinner at the Royal Lancaster to celebrate their engagement. All four of them were still busy at work. Jo and Kate drove to the hotel together, knowing that Steve and Ben would come later. The two men were now very firm friends.

The four sat in comfortable chairs in the panelled lounge, enjoying a pre-dinner drink. Jo looked from Ben to Steve thoughtfully. 'You two have been plotting,' she said. 'You keep looking at each other, hoping that the other one will start things rolling. Come on, Ben, you're the elder by four months. What is it?'

'Not going to be many secrets in our marriage, are there?' Ben sighed. 'Sometimes, Jo, you remind me of Miss Beavis, my primary school teacher. She could sense a lie before it was spoken. Yes, there is something Steve and I were talking about, just casually of course...'

'Entirely up to both of you,' Steve put in. 'It was only a vague idea but...since you're twins and very close...'

'What?' shouted Jo.

'How would you like a double wedding?' asked Ben.

There was silence for a moment. Jo looked at Kate. The idea had obviously never crossed her mind either.

'We haven't picked a date yet,' Steve said, 'and neither have you.'

'It would be, well, difficult if the two sisters got married within a few weeks of each other,' said Ben. 'Especially if they both wanted a big traditional wedding.'

'We both do,' said Kate.

'Of course, if either of you think it's a foolish idea, we'll say no more,' Ben said.

Jo picked up her glass and drank what was left in one gulp. 'I need another drink,' she said to Ben, handing him her glass. 'You and Steve go up to the bar together and get another round.'

Looking as if they had been reprieved, the two men left.

Jo eyed her sister. 'What do you think?' she asked.

'How come that pair thought of it before we did?' Kate said. 'I think it's a wonderful idea.'

'Me, too, sister.' The more she thought of it, the more Jo liked—loved the idea. They could have a double wedding!

'If you two are absolutely certain,' Jo said when the men returned, 'if it's something you both want and not just something designed to please us, then we think it's a wonderful idea.'

Ben and Steve nodded. 'It's what we both want,' Ben said. 'We had a good talk, a good think, before proposing it.'

'Then a double wedding it is,' said Kate. 'We'll have this drink to celebrate and then we'll start planning.'

'Of course, I'm the resident wedding expert,' Jo said. 'I've been through it all before, got all the plans. I've even got a wedding dress that ought to do.'

Ben and Steve looked shocked at this, but Kate laughed. 'It's just her way of showing us that she's on top of things now. Isn't it, sis?'

Jo reached over to stroke Ben's hand. 'Of course it is. In fact, I've agreed to give the dress to one of the young nurses in the department who's getting married in a bit of a hurry. She's going to wait till they've got a bit more money together and then give some to the hospital benevolent fund.'

'I think we'll leave details of dresses to you two,' said Ben. 'How d'you want us two to dress?'

They quickly decided that the two men would wear morning dress. Then, before they were called for their meal, they talked about the church, the reception, the guest list. There didn't seem to be many problems.

The sisters went to the Ladies' before the meal, and Kate said quietly, 'You're in planning mode. I know how much you enjoyed it…last time. Does this give you any worry?'

'No.' The answer was quiet but emphatic. 'I'm over everything that happened before. I didn't know that you could love someone the way I love Ben. Now, are you sure you're happy with the idea?'

'Course I am! Double wedding, half the organising. It's going to be a doddle.'

They enjoyed their meal, enjoyed each other's company. For a while they tried to talk about things other than getting married, but over the coffee Kate asked, 'What are you going to do about the house you live in now, Jo?'

Jo pondered. 'I like it,' she said. 'It's the house I know Ben from and I've got happy memories of it. I know it was planned for a marriage to Harry, but that's a ghost I've laid. Yet I don't think I want to start married life to Ben there. Unless you want to, Ben?'

'No,' he said. 'I want to sweep you off to my narrow boat. Though it was designed for one man and not a couple.'

'I am not spending a winter on a narrow boat,' Jo said firmly.

She saw Kate glance at Steve. 'Steve and I like the house very much,' Kate said. 'May we buy it off you when you're ready?'

'Certainly,' said Jo.

There was so much to do. It was now late summer and they hoped to be married next spring. They were in luck, and managed to get a date in the parish church that Jo still wanted as the place for her wedding. Then they discovered that the Royal Lancaster was building on a banqueting suite so they could be among the first to have a wedding reception there.

Events took on a momentum of their own. Andrew Kirk was delighted, but not half as delighted as his two daughters. Not only would they get to be bridesmaids but they would have to have new dresses as both of them had grown. Alice's son Michael, now fully recovered, was offered the chance to be a page boy. No one was much surprised when he turned the chance down.

Jo and Ben found a house that both of them liked—an older house that needed a lot done to the inside but was structurally sound. To Jo's surprise, Ben turned out to be a very proficient decorator. 'Practice on the narrow boat,' he told her. They were going to keep the boat as Jo was just as keen on it as Ben was.

Christmas came and went and there was the usual round of hospital festivities. But all the time there were things to do, decisions to make. Flowers, dresses, cars, guest lists, present lists, places for people to stay who were coming from some distance.

All the time the four of them were working. Their work was as engrossing, as time-consuming as it had always been. Then the wedding was two months away, a month away, ten days away.

On a Wednesday evening, Ben said, 'We get married a week on Saturday. This coming Friday night I want you to come with me and stay on the narrow boat. It might be a little chilly, but I thought we could go for a short trip on Saturday.'

'You're thinking of what happened a week before the last time I was getting married, aren't you? No need, Ben. I'm happy with what I've got. There are no ghosts to lay.'

'We'll still have a trip,' he said. 'It was on the narrow boat that I first got to know you well.'

In fact, the ghost of Harry had been well and truly laid. He had apparently gone back to Australia, and no one had heard of or from him. 'I hope he's happy there,' Jo said sincerely to her sister.

It was their wedding day and it was going to be fine. The first thing booked was an early trip to the hairdresser's. Jo and Kate went down there in their track-suits. When they returned they found Penny Kirk and Alice Benson waiting for them. Each was going to be a matron of honour and they would have a little girl each as bridesmaid. They had decided that with a joint wedding more than two attendants each would be excessive. Jen and Jan Kirk were still half-convinced that the whole ceremony had been arranged so that they could wear their new dresses.

Jo and Kate had dresses made for them in the same material but in different patterns. The material was a rich ivory brocade and both dresses were full length. Jo had tried on her dress already, of course, but when finally she put it on to be married... 'It feels different today, doesn't it?' she said to Kate, the slightest tremor in her voice.

'Yes,' said Kate, obviously feeling the same, 'it does feel different.'

Kate was being given away by John Bellis, an old friend from America. He had flown over, partly for the wedding and partly, Kate told Jo she suspected, because of his interest in Vanessa Welsh, Steve's practice manager. Jo was being given away by Andrew Kirk.

When Jo had awoken at six that morning, it had seemed as if the time would never pass. But then there had been a bewildering amount of last-minute jobs, last-minute decisions and in the end they didn't even have time to sit down. Then it was time. Everyone was dressed, there were four old Rolls Royces outside and the neighbours had come out to see them go.

Jo kissed her sister, checking to make sure that her

make-up hadn't smudged. Then she walked down to her car.

She was driven through the streets she had known since her childhood, but this time they seemed different. People turned to look at her. They stopped outside the church, she stepped from the car and Alice carefully arranged her gown, adjusted her veil. She walked through the lych gate. It seemed that those from the hospital who weren't in the church were waiting outside for her.

It was dark in the church porch and it took a moment for her eyes to get accustomed to the gloom. There was a last fussing by the matrons of honour, then Jo took a deep breath and was ready. From inside came the exciting booming of a piece of music Ben particularly liked—'The Arrival of the Queen of Sheba'.

Jo was the elder sister by ten minutes so she went first. She stepped into the church. Ahead of her she saw Ben, and his best man, Rob Simpson, step into the aisle.

She was going to marry Ben Franklin. She was the happiest woman in the world.

MILLS & BOON®

Makes any time special™

Mills & Boon publish 29 new titles every month. Select from...

Modern Romance™ Tender Romance™

Sensual Romance™

Medical Romance™ Historical Romance™

MAT2

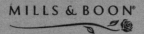

FREE!

4 Books
and a surprise gift!

We would like to take this opportunity to thank you for reading this Mills & Boon® book by offering you the chance to take FOUR more specially selected titles from the Medical Romance™ series absolutely FREE! We're also making this offer to introduce you to the benefits of the Reader Service™—

- ★ FREE home delivery
- ★ FREE gifts and competitions
- ★ FREE monthly Newsletter
- ★ Books available before they're in the shops
- ★ Exclusive Reader Service discounts

Accepting these FREE books and gift places you under no obligation to buy; you may cancel at any time, even after receiving your free shipment. Simply complete your details below and return the entire page to the address below. *You don't even need a stamp!*

YES! Please send me 4 free Medical Romance books and a surprise gift. I understand that unless you hear from me, I will receive 6 superb new titles every month for just £2.49 each, postage and packing free. I am under no obligation to purchase any books and may cancel my subscription at any time. The free books and gift will be mine to keep in any case.

MIZEB

Ms/Mrs/Miss/Mr ....Initials..
BLOCK CAPITALS PLEASE

Surname...

Address..

....

....Postcode ....

Send this whole page to:
UK: The Reader Service, FREEPOST CN8I, Croydon, CR9 3WZ
EIRE: The Reader Service, PO Box 4546, Kilcock, County Kildare (stamp required)